BEYOND REVENGE

ART OF PAYBACK
BOOK 2

DAN PETROSINI

1

READING CAPTIONS WAS ANNOYING, BUT THE NETFLIX SERIES was captivating. The drama covered a drug deal gone wrong. A couple of parcels of coke were handed off, and the scene switched to a woman embracing a young boy. They were crying.

The lady looked exactly like Mrs. Morse. I burped up a mouthful of the tacos I'd eaten earlier. Stomach churning, I hopped off the couch and ran into the bathroom.

I spit into the sink and put the faucet on. Rinsing, my stomach rumbled. I sat on the bowl and shut my eyes.

The searing movie in my head started again.

There I was, walking home from school. I turned the corner onto my block and paused.

A crowd of neighbors was talking to a uniformed officer. Someone had her head in her hands. It was Mrs. Morse.

My throat tightened. Taking a couple steps forward, I counted houses. Ours was the fifth one from the corner.

I squinted. A cop was standing in front of the steps to our home. Heart pounding, I started running.

A house away, I could see our front door. It was open.

Slowing down, I asked the cop, "What are you doing here?"

"Move along, kid, this is a police matter."

"But this is my house. Where's my mom?"

"Hold on, son."

The cop looked like he was about to enter the gates of hell. "Sarge. Sarge!" He stepped toward two cops near a patrol car. "This kid, he lives here."

I bolted up the stairs, two at a time.

"Hey, you can't go in there!"

My mother was on the floor. Two men were kneeling over her. A halo of blood encircled her head. My voice cracked, "Mom!"

Startled, the cops scrambled to their feet. They stepped in front of me, turning me around. "You have to get out of here."

"Mommy! Mommy! Get up!"

"Get him outside!"

A pair of hands lifted me. "No! Leave me alone!"

They carried me out, handing me off to Mrs. Morse. She took my hand and wiped the tears from her face with her other one. "Come on. Be strong—"

I tried to wriggle free. "I want to see Mommy."

"You can't, sweetheart. Not right now."

"When? When can I see her?"

"Your daddy's on his way home from work. He'll tell you when."

"What happened to her? Is she going to be, okay? She was bleeding and everything."

"They're doing what they can."

"She wasn't moving."

Mrs. Morse's chin quivered. A tear rolled down her cheek.

My mouth was bone-dry. "Is she dead?"

"Here comes your daddy."

Dad's face was as white as snow. "Dad! Something happened to Mommy!"

He put up a hand and started talking to a policeman. I broke free from Mrs. Morse's grasp. Taking a step toward my father, a movement at the top of the stairs caught my attention.

Someone was backing out of the front door. He was holding one end of a stretcher. Light bounced off the shiny black bag on the gurney. My stomach snaked; Mom was in the bag.

Dad tugged at my hand. "Come on, you shouldn't see this."

"I want to stay with Mommy!"

"We'll see her later."

"Where? Where? At the funeral parlor?"

My dad's chin shook. He turned away and his shoulders heaved.

"Dad? Are you all right?"

Mr. Amato put his arm around Dad. "We're so sorry, Bill."

Amato's wife squeezed my hand. "Why don't you come over to our house for a little while?"

I shook her off. Crying, I followed the stretcher to the back of the ambulance.

"Who did this to my mom? Who? Why? Why did they do this?"

A cop holding open the doors to the emergency vehicle said, "Don't worry, kid. We know who it was. We'll get him before it turns dark."

I pushed past the EMT and reached for the bag. I felt her leg. It was like a piece of pipe.

"Dad! They know who did it." The pounding between my eyes quickened. "Who, who hurt my mommy?"

The details of the day my mom was killed were vivid. It was weird because the following week, including the funeral, was a blur. The only thing I remembered from the wake was cops walking in asking to see my father.

Dad met with them in the lobby. Whispering circulated around the room, crescendoing as Mrs. Morse knelt by my chair. "The police caught the man who did this to your mother."

The bastard was Larry Boyd. And he was out on bail when he did it, even though he'd brutally beaten two other women. It was the first proof of how broken the system was. After Dad died, from slow-motion suicide by the bottle, I was tossed into foster care.

Losing your parents and getting shuffled around was tough enough, but being beaten in foster care consumed me with the need for revenge. After escaping the abuse, my first target was Mr. Bryant, the foster father who gave me the three-inch scar behind my ear.

Things didn't work out, and just like the man who shot my mother, he died before I could kill him myself. After losing everything, I was robbed, again.

The frustration clouded my life. I tried to move on, taking a job as an investigator with a lawyer named Ray Larson. It was there that an outlet for getting even presented itself.

Going after the system that screwed me over was impossible. What evolved was part business and part what I hoped was therapy, seeking revenge on behalf of others.

2

————

Celebration Park was getting busy. Weaving my way through the early dinner crowd, I waited near Cousin's Maine Lobster truck.

Al Ventura, a lawyer who fed me work, came around a turn, and I jumped in the food order line.

I extended my hand. "Hey Al, how are you?"

"Good, Beck."

"Hungry?"

He nodded. "I love their crab rolls."

"They're good, but the lobster rolls are out of this world."

"I like them both. Say, how was your trip?"

"Relaxing. I was down in the Keys for two weeks, and then Laura and I went to the Bahamas for six days."

"The Bahamas? How's things going with her?"

"Okay."

"I thought you might have found a life partner. Was I mistaken? Is something wrong?"

"Nothing."

"You can tell me. I've been married and would still be if Lee Ann hadn't died. What's going on?"

"Laura's always asking questions. She wants to know everything, my family, what I do for a living, blah, blah, blah. That's not me. I'm private."

"A partnership is a give-and-take. It's natural to want to know everything you can about someone you're in a relationship with. You shouldn't shut down. Find a way to give her a little at a time, say, about your family. It's part of who you are."

The last part was truer than I cared to admit. "I get it. But what about what I do? Nobody can know details of—"

"You're one of the smarter guys I know. Create a story. Something believable, and it'll be over."

"I was doing that but tripped up at the end of our vacation."

"Get back on track. She's good for you. You have to work at it."

"I'll try."

"Good. Did you stay at Larson's house in Lyford Cay?"

"Yeah, what a setup. He's like, right next to where Sean Connery used to live."

"I've been there once. It's a magical place."

"Yeah, maybe it was being in the Keys for a couple of weeks beforehand, but it got boring. Laura is happy sitting on the beach reading, but I get antsy. I went fishing, and it was cool, but you can't go every day."

"A lot of guys do."

"That's not for me, I got to keep busy."

"Laura must have loved it."

"She did, but money isn't important to her; she works three days a week from home and barely makes rent."

"Don't complain, that's a good trait for a partner to have."

"I know."

"She's a patient advocate, right?"

"Yes, when an insurance company gives somebody the runaround on a prescription, she tries to get them covered."

Ventura smiled. "How about that? You both help people you don't know."

We put our orders in and made small talk until the food was ready.

Carrying our dinner to a high-top table, Ventura said, "You ready to get back to work?"

"Definitely. Tell me about the situation you mentioned."

The strings of overhead lights swayed as a breeze blew off the canal. Ventura wiped his mouth. "Man, that is so good."

"What about the kid who was—"

"It's a sad case. One of the saddest things I've ever come across."

I set my roll down and looked him in the eye.

He swallowed and said, "Okay, okay. In short, a child was taken from her parents by the state."

"Child Protection Services?"

"Yes."

I picked up my lobster. "How old was she?"

"The kid was under a year old."

"They suspected the parents of abuse?"

He nodded. "They arrested both of them when tests revealed the baby had a fracture."

"The authorities thought the parents beat the kid?"

"Either that or serious neglect."

I pushed my half-eaten roll away. "How did this start?"

"I'm not really certain. Someone reported the situation to the child welfare department."

"If nothing was going on, why would anyone report them?"

Mouth full, Ventura shrugged.

"There had to be something there, no?"

"It's complicated. The parents came to me for legal advice. They wanted to take the county or state to court for what happened. I really felt for them."

"Why didn't you sue if they were screwed over?"

"I know you don't like secondhand information. And given the circumstances, it's best you hear it directly from the parents."

People were parked on the grass ballfields. I joined a stream of people trudging into East Naples Community Park. Anonymity was something I treasured, but this was overkill.

The name of the Jimmy Buffet-inspired resort, Margaritaville, was all over the signage. The Fort Myers hotel complex was wasting no time etching its name on Southwest Florida. Salted or not, drinking a margarita was no way to get to the pickleball championship.

I breezed past dozens of courts; pickleball players of all ages were competing to move onto the main stage. Signage touting a live CBS broadcast of the finals hung over the main thoroughfare. Pickleball on TV? How much prize money was at stake?

Inside a tented area, the Dubers were seated at a picnic table. As I approached, the husband put his coffee cup down. He had good instincts.

I stuck my hand out. "Good to meet you, Mr. Duber. I'm Beck."

His pale blue shirt had a frayed collar. "Same here. I'm Jim, and this is Sarah."

Her hand was white and soft. "Thanks for coming."

"Ma'am." I swung my leg over the bench and sat.

Sarah reached for her husband's hand and whispered, "Can you help us?"

"I don't know, but I'd like to know what happened."

She looked at Jim, then said, "Okay. Um, Katy was, is, our first child. We tried for, like five years—"

Jim corrected her, "Almost seven."

Sarah nodded. "Yeah, we did the whole fertility thing like, two times—"

"Three times, what a waste of money."

"Yeah, money we don't have."

I said, "Your daughter, Katy, was a surprise, then?"

Sarah beamed. "Totally unexpected. I mean, I prayed for a baby, and it worked, but yeah, we were, like, totally surprised. I mean, it was great."

"We had a whole list of people praying for us, and God blessed us with her."

"When was she born?"

"It's hard to believe she's going to be two in a couple of months."

"Happy birthday to her. Now, when did the trouble start?"

The mother said, "Katy is a great baby, but she seemed to always be sick. I remember she just turned ten months, and one morning, she started throwing up. It wasn't real bad, but we called the doctor. She told us to keep an eye on her, and if it continued, to bring her in that afternoon. She said to be careful of dehydration and to make sure she drank enough—"

"Sarah called me, and I picked up some Pedialyte at Walmart."

His wife continued, "I didn't like the way she was and brought her to the pediatrician. We couldn't make up what happened after that. Right, hon?"

Jim said, "It's been one long nightmare. We should be on one of those *Dateline* shows or something."

3

———————

THE FALSE DRAMA OF *DATELINE*'S HOST HAD TURNED ME OFF years ago. "So, you took her to the doctor, and what happened?"

"It was like, eleven, and Jim had to go to work. He's a cook at New York, New York Pizza. It was no big deal. I mean, she was sick, but I could handle her alone."

He hung his head. "I should've been there with you. Sarah called me, hysterical, and I almost got in two accidents rushing there."

"Tell me what went on at the doctor's."

Sarah said, "Well, they checked her vitals and stuff, and they were gonna put her on an IV for liquids, but they took her for an ultrasound to see if she had swallowed something or whatever. To tell you the truth, I can't remember what they said after they accused us."

"What did they accuse you of?"

"Child abuse. Can you believe it? What bull . . . uh, dinky."

Bull dinky? "What did they find that made them think it was abuse?"

"Well, it started when they found Katy had a fracture in one of her ribs, on her left side. They asked me what happened, and I said nothing. They asked if she had fallen or if we had dropped her. Can you imagine?"

"What happened next?"

"I told them she didn't fall and that nobody dropped her. They told me to wait outside, and I asked why. They said I had to. I didn't want to leave Katy, but I did, even though she was scared." Sarah's eyes teared up and she picked up a napkin.

Jim dug a fingernail into the table, saying, "They called the frigging police, and everything went downhill from there."

"Why?"

Sarah said, "Well, they said they did more scans and found Katy had three other fractures: two in her legs, and one in Katy's forearm. I mean, I couldn't believe it; there was no way she could have gotten that. We're always together." She closed her eyes for a couple of seconds, then said, "They asked me if we'd hit her. It was unreal. I mean, she's helpless. Who would hurt their own baby?"

Unfortunately, there were many who'd crossed that line. The question was whether the Dubers had. "And they called the police, thinking someone was abusing your daughter?"

She nodded. "Not someone, either me or Jim. When I said we didn't do anything, they tried to see if I'd turn on Jim. Like I'd protect him if he did something to Katy. Can you imagine?"

"Sarah called me, and I had to leave work. They questioned us for an hour, and the next thing we knew, Child Protection Services shows up."

"None of them were nice people, right, hon? Especially that Simone Jackson. She treated us like criminals. A witch is what she is."

"What happened next?"

Sarah's face clouded. "They wouldn't let us take Katy home. They took our daughter from us. It was like from a movie or something. We tried to explain we'd done nothing and would never hurt our baby, but they didn't want to hear it."

She dabbed her eyes before continuing, "They made us wait in another room, and the next thing we knew, Katy was gone. We were desperate. I begged them to tell us where she was, but they refused. They said to call the next day, in the afternoon, after Katy was examined by a supposed expert on child abuse. Then they'd let us know if we could visit her or not. That Jackson woman smiled when she said any visit would have to be supervised. And that's when, I, I blacked out."

"You fainted?"

Jim nodded. "Thank God I was next to her. I caught her before she hit the floor."

***

Why was I feeling so crappy? I had a new case to explore and good leads on a couple of others. Usually, that kind of excitement produced energy.

What was going on? I pushed away the thought that it could be the Duber case. It was an important case but depressing and too close to home.

I headed for the refrigerator; a good meal might change the vibe.

Cool air from the fridge escaped as I stared inside. Nothing inspiring. Slamming it shut, I headed to the lanai. Peeling off my T-shirt, I jumped into the pool wearing my shorts.

It felt good. Like ice cream or when it snowed as a kid, your mood changed immediately. I toweled off and changed. Going into the family room, I saw a couple outside walking by. They were holding hands.

The blues crept back in. "Come here, Toby." My dog raised his head but stayed in his bed.

I plopped onto the couch and reviewed my last victory, the Petersen case. Concocting such an elaborate scheme had taken a ton of time and money, but we pulled it off and it felt good. For a day or so. Bringing it back up didn't even evoke a quick smile.

Palming my phone, I punched in a number. "Hey, Laura."

"Oh, hi, Beck."

We hadn't seen each other since getting back from the Bahamas. "What are you doing?"

"Nothing. I just got back from Grace Place."

She tutored kids English. "Nice. So, how have you been?"

"You know, keeping busy. And you?"

"Everything is pretty good."

"That's nice."

"It's been too long. You want to get together?"

"Today?"

"Yeah, I'm thinking of whipping up one of my world-famous feasts."

She scoffed. "World famous?"

"You know, if more people had a chance to taste my master-pieces, I'd get a show on the Cooking Channel."

"You make a world-class mess; I'll give you that."

"Aw, come on. I'm not that bad."

"Oh, yes, you are."

"All those big-time chefs have a cleanup crew. I'm at a disadvantage."

"Poor Beck, has to clean up after himself."

I chuckled. "What do you say? Come over around five. We'll hang out and I'll make you the best dinner you ever had."

She hesitated. "I don't know."

"It'll be fun."

"What are you making?"

"Whatever you want. I'll go to Whole Foods. You liked lobster tails and grilled veggies, right?"

As soon as it tumbled out of my mouth, I regretted it. Right before we left the Bahamas, I made it for her, and we had a major-league fight. "Or, I could make my tomato sauce and chicken meatballs, or honey garlic pork chops with—"

"Okay."

"Great. What do you feel like?"

"Surprise me. What time should I be there?"

"Come at five. If that works for you."

"That's perfect."

"Great." I punched the air as I hung up. What was dinner going to be? I could make the sauce, or maybe she'd like the pork chops better.

Deciding to call an audible at the grocery store, my phone rang. It was Prosecutor O'Leary. He wanted to see me about a politician. My sauce took a couple of hours to simmer; it'd have to be pork chops tonight. I headed out.

4

———

O'Leary was sitting under the lone umbrella at Aurelio's Family Pizzeria. When had the eatery moved to the Coastland Shopping Center?

"Hey, how's it going?"

The prosecutor grabbed my hand. "It's interesting, to say the least. And you?"

"Pretty well. You know, I have never been to this place."

"It's a chain, but they make a good pie."

"From Chicago, right?"

"Yes, the original place went up in 1950. Do you want to share a pie?"

"I'm only having one slice. I have dinner plans."

"I'll order one anyway. Whatever is left, I'll take back to the office."

As a young server came out of the restaurant, I said, "Sounds good. How about a margarita style one?"

"That's my favorite." He ordered the pizza and a couple glasses of water.

I asked, "What's going on in the prosecutor's office?"

"Busy, but nothing out of the ordinary."

"What's with the politician you mentioned?"

O'Leary waited for the waitress to set down red-pepper and cheese shakers.

"I think it's perfect for you. Shouldn't be too difficult, but it's important."

It was always easy when you didn't have to do it yourself. "Sounds interesting."

"It's perfect for you."

Why didn't people get to the point? "You going to tell me what it is?"

"Woman's name is Hannah Ruta. She worked in Marty Kravitz's office."

"The congressman?"

"Exactly. Kravitz never met a camera he didn't like."

That described ninety percent of the clowns in Washington. "Wasn't there a scandal involving him, about two years back?"

"More like three years ago. A whistleblower reached out to the office of the congressional ombuds and—"

"Ombuds?"

"Gender neutral, buddy. Anyway, the whistleblower was Hannah Ruta. She alerted them on what she believed was an ongoing scheme to siphon money from campaign contributions for personal use by Kravitz. We're talking real money; Ruta said at least five million was moved over a six-year period."

"Sounds exactly like what goes on in DC."

"Sadly, it does. And even more frustrating was the ombuds supposedly launched an investigation, but it went nowhere. Kravitz didn't even get the slightest sanction."

"Here's your pizza, gentlemen." The server dropped napkins, plates, and a work of art composed of carbs.

We slid pieces onto our plates. I said, "They whitewashed it?"

O'Leary used a knife and fork to cut off a corner. "It's the way congress works. There's a fatal flaw built into the system; congress is in charge of overseeing itself."

I folded my slice. "No wonder it's so corrupt."

"You know, when I was a kid wondering what to do for a living, I never thought about politics. I thought there was no money in it. Boy, was I wrong."

"Amen. The pizza is good."

"I knew you'd like it."

"Looking into a congressman is not something I'm particularly interested in."

"It's not the corruption piece. After Ruta blew the whistle, word leaked out it was her."

"What a surprise."

"No doubt it was on purpose. She was fired and hasn't been able to get a meaningful job since."

"Kravitz blackballed her?"

"That's what it looks like. He spread all kinds of rumors about Ruta. Kravitz basically ruined her life."

Reaching for another slice, I pulled my hand back. "She didn't fight back?"

"Ruta lives in Collier and worked at the office Kravitz has in town, but we got smacked down on jurisdiction. It's really a federal matter. Besides, we don't have the resources to go after a congressman."

Wiping my mouth, I smiled. "This could be a fun one."

The doorbell rang. I stuffed a cutting board and a pot in the dishwasher and swept broccoli fragments into the sink with a towel.

"Hey." I took a six-pack of cans from Laura. "You didn't have to bring anything."

"I had a Moscow mule with Susan the other day and thought I'd try these. They're premixed."

I pecked her cheek. She looked great. "What's in it?"

"Vodka, ginger beer, lime, and some other stuff."

"I'll find out and make fresh ones for you."

"You don't have to. I barely drank one the whole night."

"You want one now?"

"No, not yet. It smells delicious. What are you making?"

"Honey garlic pork chops, roasted red potatoes, and broccoli."

"Wow. You went all out."

"There's no dessert, so you'll have to do."

She smiled. "We'll see about that."

I wrapped my arms around her. "You smell great. I'm glad you came."

"You know me, I wouldn't miss a free meal. Especially one from a world-famous chef."

I released her. "Don't be a wiseass."

She smiled and said, "What can I do? Set the table?"

"You want to eat inside or out?"

"You like it outside better."

"Only if that's okay with you. I'm cool either way."

While clearing the table, Laura said, "That was so good, I ate too much."

"Glad you enjoyed it."

"You want to take a little walk? It'll help me digest."

"Sure. Toby needs to go out as well."

Laura hooked her arm around mine and Toby led the way. A block away, a couple pushing a stroller were headed toward us. I shortened the leash as we drew nearer.

Laura said, "Hi, there."

I stepped into the street while Laura peeked in the stroller. "Oh my God. She's adorable."

"Thanks."

"How old is she?"

"Eight months tomorrow."

"Well, happy birthday. Beck, look at this little darling."

I handed off the leash. "She is cute. What's her name?"

"Catherine."

"Beautiful. Take care."

We went our separate ways. The baby had the same name as the Duber kid. Toby sniffed a bush before doing his business. We walked two blocks in silence.

Laura said, "Are you okay?"

I nodded.

"What's the matter?"

"Nothing."

"It's not nothing. You got quiet all of a sudden."

"I don't know."

"Was it the baby? Are you afraid of having kids?"

"No. That's not it."

She stopped and gave me a look. It was bordering on trouble. "Then what is it?"

"The baby reminded me of someone."

"Who?"

The questioning machine gun was loaded. "Just some kid."

"From your childhood?"

I shook my head. "It's work related."

"What's it about?"

"A baby that was taken from her parents."

"Oh, my God. A kidnapping?"

It was in the public records so not confidential. "No. Social services accused them of abuse, and it wasn't true. It's a real mess."

"That's terrible, the poor parents. What are you doing for them?"

"At this point, I'm not sure. A lawyer is collecting information, and we'll see."

"They should be sued for a zillion dollars, make sure it never happens again."

I pulled her close and kissed her. My hips ground into hers. "Let's turn around."

5

Like many personal injury lawyers, Claude Davis ran annoying ads on TV. His face was also plastered all over billboards, but Davis became famous for an infamous case that led to a TV documentary.

Davis's office was in a strip center near Naples Airport. The lines on his face were deep but his smile warm.

His large hand enveloped mine. "A friend of Ray's is a friend of mine."

My lawyer buddy, Ray Larson, had a stellar reputation. "Thanks, I appreciate your time."

He lifted a stack of files off a chair and set them on the floor by his desk. "Sit, sit."

"You look busy."

"I pretty much take the cases I want to work on these days. Ray said you needed some info on child advocacy."

"Yes. I figured with your experience with the Green case, you could offer some insight."

"I've been in practice close to thirty years and handled hundreds of cases. But one case makes it on TV, and that's all anybody wants to talk about."

"No, no. This is different. I saw the documentary, and that family got screwed over, but they made it seem like you believe failures in the system are pervasive."

"Pervasive is not the correct way to characterize it. There are some good people in Collier's child protection system, but it's far from perfect."

"Got it. Can I give you some background on a particular case?"

"Sure."

I finished telling him about the Dubers by saying, "And they got totally screwed. And to top it off, the Dubers have limited resources and had to borrow money to pay for the lawyers they needed."

"I presume they tried suing for damages?"

"Yeah, but they signed—"

He finished the sentence, "They signed a waiver so they could see their child."

"Exactly. I don't know how the agency gets away with tactics like that. I mean, you'd sign anything to see your kid after they've been taken from you."

"They designed the system, and the courts allow them discretion. Too much, in my opinion."

"The Netflix case, that was different from the one I'm looking at—"

"They both involved charges of parental abuse. In your case, it was a physical issue, and in the Green case, they thought the parents were overtreating and medicating the child. They thought the girl's pain was mentally fabricated. End of the day, there are similarities."

"The woman who made the decision to take the Duber baby was a Simone Jackson."

Davis frowned.

"You know her?"

"Unfortunately, I do. After I managed to get the Greens reunited, and before the documentary was filmed, parents started reaching out. I took on two cases before I realized that sector of the legal system wasn't something I could stomach. It's important work, but it's not a good fit for me. I get too emotional. It hurts the work and my sleep."

Did he have personal experience like I did? "I get it. What can you tell me about Simone Jackson?"

"Where to start with her? Jackson is self-righteous. The woman either believes she is right or can't accept that she may have been wrong. I don't know everything, but in my opinion she's vindictive, and that's where the most harm occurs."

"Can you explain that?"

"It's one thing to take action in the name of protecting a child, but when evidence surfaces proving the parent or parents were innocent of any abuse or neglect, you should acknowledge it and do what is necessary to close the case with as little damage as possible."

"And Jackson doesn't do that?"

"She seems to consciously double down, taking a vindictive stance against the parents who fight back."

"Can you provide an example?"

"Sure. What happened to the Wilson family illustrates this perfectly. The Wilsons' youngest child, Emerald, who was two years old at the time, climbed onto the couch and fell. He hit his shoulder on the corner of a table, opening a gash. It wouldn't stop bleeding, and the parents took him to the emergency room. They patched him up, if I recall. It required a couple of stitches, but during the process the ER doctor noticed several discolorations on his body."

"He notified the authorities?"

"Yes. Which is protocol, and I don't have a problem with that. However, to cut right to it, the agent in charge of the response was Jackson. She ordered that the parents be separated from the child until a determination by a pediatrician with abuse experience could perform an examination. Well, putting aside the fact that the doctor, an Anil Khan, has a reputation of being overly cautious, he determined it likely abuse or that a series of falls were at fault, and the police were called."

"Even though it could have been from falling, they called the police?"

"Yes. Jackson's notes glossed over it, notating that if it were a series of falls, she believed it amounted to negligence on the part of the parents. The parents were arrested, and their other child was removed from their home as well. That's when I got the call."

Davis nodded. "What a mess. I can see why you don't want these kinds of cases."

"I immediately ordered examinations by two separate pediatricians. Both determined that the child has a rare blood disorder, causing him to bruise easier than normal."

"Nobody knew this before?"

"Apparently not. We obtained the medical records from the child's pediatrician, and there was nothing in it, but it wasn't as if the child would bruise extraordinarily easily."

"What happened then?"

"The charges were dropped, and Emerald was reunited with his parents. But Jackson wouldn't release the other kid from foster care."

"What? Why not?"

"Pardon my French, but it was pure bullshit. The kid had a welt on his back. Jackson said it could have been from being beaten. The parents and the child himself said he'd gotten it at the playground when he fell off a swing. She wouldn't release him until they had a child psychologist interview the child. It took two days."

"You think it was retribution?"

"Most definitely. At the risk of sounding silly, Jackson is a power-hungry Nazi."

"There shouldn't be one person making such important decisions."

"She is the worst offender, but Doctor Khan and the administrator, a wimp named Jim Clyde, let Jackson walk all over them."

"You said you were involved in another problematic case."

6

———

After talking to Davis, the lawyer who had gone up against Jackson and Child Protection Services, it was time to speak with Jason Grimes, the attorney who had represented the Dubers in the battle to get their child back.

Just before Route 41, I slipped off Immokalee Road, into the Riverchase Shopping Center.

Grimes Family Law was tucked away in a low-slung building next to Cardinale Dentistry. I stepped into a small glassed-in foyer and rang the bell. A man in his twenties lifted his head and came around his desk.

"How can I help you?"

"I have an appointment with Mr. Grimes. My name is Beck."

"One minute, Mr. Beck."

He poked his head into a doorway and stepped aside as a tall, lanky man came out of the office.

Jason Grimes was in his mid-forties. Wearing a long-sleeved white shirt and a blue tie, Grimes had recently gotten a haircut. "Mr. Beck, nice to meet you."

We shook hands and I followed him into an office lined with photographs. "You have a large family."

Grimes slid behind his desk, saying, "Those are all clients."

"They must like you."

"When you're able to reunite a family, it's an emotional tie that lasts. The problem is you can't win every one of these cases, and even when you do, it unfortunately takes too long."

"I can't imagine what these parents have to go through."

"A nightmare, and it is extremely difficult on the children. They're not equipped, emotionally or intellectually, to deal with the separation or the charges leveled against the parents."

"Kids are tougher than you think; they adapt."

"I'm a lawyer, not a psychologist, but everything I've seen leads me to believe the experiences leave scars, and the chances are they're permanent."

I was tempted to ask him if he'd represented any children in a legal action against a foster parent. "Kids are resilient, but I get it. It's far from optimal."

"It may be that a child as young as the Dubers' won't be impacted as badly, but the parents? Overprotective would be an understatement."

"I get that. What can you tell me about their experience?"

"What exactly is your role, Mr. Beck?"

"Like a journalist, I look to shine a light on situations that need it. Families like the Dubers need to know there are people who care, even when the justice system fails."

"I'm not sure the justice system is what failed here. There's a lot of gray in the child protection world, and when you add in the human element, it can easily go awry."

"Awry is an interesting way to describe what happened to the Dubers. It sounds unintentional, and it may be the case in most situations, but I've looked around some, and a common denominator is Simone Jackson. Isn't that more like malpractice?"

Grimes smoothed his tie. "Off the record?"

"Everything between us is off the record, Mr. Grimes."

"Good. In the cases I've been involved in, I'd say Ms. Jackson's behavior is less than ideal."

"Less than ideal? That's it?"

"Some might classify it as tyrannical."

"Can we start at the beginning of the Duber case?"

"I received a call from Jim Duber. He'd been recommended by a colleague who handles criminal law. Mr. Duber sounded desperate, and when he mentioned Simone Jackson, I made room on my calendar. He and Sarah came in late that afternoon. At that time, the child had been taken from them for several days."

"Why did they wait to get legal help?"

"It was based on the belief that they hadn't done anything wrong and hadn't abused their child. They believed it would work out and acquiesced to everything asked of them. But, as is generally the case, they began to feel the system was set on punishing them for no reason."

"How were they when you met with them?"

"They were understandably emotional. Sarah broke down several times explaining their side of the story."

"You checked into them before taking action?"

"While we're bound to represent our clients to the best of our ability, it doesn't mean we accept what they say as gospel. Law enforcement had nothing on either of the parents, and the pediatrician had taken care of the child since birth and had seen her regularly. There wasn't even a whisper of impropriety."

"What did you do?"

"We petitioned and were granted an evaluation by an independent pediatrician who discovered the blood disorder."

"Were the Dubers reunited immediately?"

He exhaled heavily. "No. Child Protection fought the release, but at an emergency hearing the court ruled for release."

"What a crazy situation."

"And all the time that this was going on, the Dubers did whatever was asked of them. They even enrolled in parenting and anger classes. When they were finally allowed to visit their child under supervision, they were patted down like common criminals."

"It's hard to believe."

"And to top it off, three months after the case was resolved, they received a notice that the investigation into the allegations of child abuse against them was found to be"—he made air quotes—"valid. The notice said both parents were being put on a child abuse registry until Katy turned eighteen. They had twenty days to file an appeal. We had to drop everything to make sure the appeal was filed in time."

"That's unbelievable. They were covering their asses?"

"Maybe, but either way, it's humiliating and degrading. And so unnecessary."

7

———

I PUT ASIDE THE CHILD PROTECTION CASE TO MEET THE WOMAN that Kravitz, the politician, had seemingly screwed over.

Hanna Ruta was seated at one of Parmesan Pete's outdoor tables. Approaching, I waved. She stood.

"Nice to meet you, Hannah." She was several inches taller than me. Her hairstyle needed updating; it made her look older than the forty-nine her DMV record stated.

"Thank you for coming to see me."

"No problem. Believe it or not, this is the first time I've been here."

"Really? The owner is from New York- -Brooklyn, I think, just like you."

"Close, I was born in Jersey."

"Oh, your accent sounds like a New York one."

I had an accent? "Right next door to each other."

Ruta had a nice smile. She picked up a menu. "If you like chicken parm, everybody says theirs is the best."

"You never had it?"

She wrinkled her nose. "I watch what I eat."

"It shows."

"Having something like that for lunch would ruin the day for me."

"Me too. I'm going with the beet salad with shrimp."

"That sounds good."

The waiter took our orders, gathered the menus, and left.

"Tell me about Kravitz."

Ruta hissed, "He's pure evil. My eyes are open. I know politicians are full of themselves and lie when it suits them, but Kravitz is in a class by himself."

It was doubtful he was alone. "How long were you working for him?"

"Almost ten years. After he won his third term, he climbed the ranks and was appointed to a couple of key committees. I was working for County Commissioner Leahy, and a friend said Kravitz was hiring and I'd be a good fit. I enjoyed working for Leahy and wasn't looking, but Leahy heard about it and told me I would be silly to pass up the opportunity."

"More money?"

"Yes, but at the time it was more the position. Like an idiot, I thought the whole Washington thing was exciting, you know, working on national issues and all. Boy, was I wrong. We didn't work on anything but raising money and getting Kravitz reelected."

"Running every two years is a joke. As soon as they win, they're campaigning for the next term."

"That's exactly what I experienced. It's a game, a big con. People think their congressperson is working for them. Nothing could be further from the truth. It's complete nonsense. The main thing is raising money. Eighty percent of the time they're meeting with businesses who want something done. These companies make donations to get what they want."

"Pay for play."

"Unfortunately, that's what it is."

"What made you report what you discovered?"

"I couldn't live with myself anymore. The main responsibility of my job was tracking donors, classifying them into groups, who was increasing the amounts, whether there was a policy attached to it, and who else we could target in that sphere. Also, I tracked how we were raising money, quarter over quarter and year over year. Looking at things like the types of events, the location, any detail that led to a good haul."

"Was it always going up?"

Ruta nodded. "Kravitz was very good at opening wallets."

"It's a trait most politicians seem to have."

"They sure do. But something didn't make sense. It really jumped off the page a couple of months after the last election cycle I was a part of. Expenses usually dropped significantly in the first quarter of the year after the election, you know, no advertising, temporary workers being let go, that kind of thing."

"You had access to how Kravitz was spending the money?"

"Not originally. Kravitz walled things off. But I'd been there so long, I was able to ask questions of two other staffers without raising any concerns."

"What did you find?"

"The first thing I saw was a payment to a company named Star Island Properties. It was eighty-five thousand dollars. When I asked what it was for, they said they held a weeklong strategy meeting for top donors in Miami. I hadn't heard of such a meeting, and I checked into it." She frowned. "That company only rents high-end homes on Star Island. It didn't feel right because Mary, Kravitz's wife, said they were going on a two-week vacation to an island."

I scoffed.

She said, "Yeah, they went to an island, a private island where the likes of Madonna and Gloria Estefan live. And the campaign paid for it."

"You're sure of that?"

"Without a doubt. And that was only the beginning. His daughter lives in New York City. Guess who is paying her rent? When I asked about a payment to a company identified as NYLA, I was told it was a media outfit doing ads on social platforms. But I found out it's a New York City luxury apartment outfit. The payments were annotated L Kravitz 18B. His daughter is Linda, and her apartment is 18B."

"They didn't make much of an effort to hide it."

She nodded. "The arrogance is what really ticked me off. In private, I went to Kravitz and told him it looked like some campaign money was used for personal purposes. I said the best thing to do was to repay the fund. He said he'd look into it, but I knew he wasn't going to do anything. Next thing I know, my access was restricted. Since I was there so long, I knew most of the staff a long time. Two of them secretly told me they were instructed to stay away from me, that I wasn't a team player and was a spy for the Anton campaign, Kravitz's opponent in the next election."

"And that's why you blew the whistle?"

"Like I said, the whole thing bothered me. I tried to make him clean it up, but he forced my hand. I had no choice."

"What happened when Kravitz became aware you'd reported him?"

"He circled the wagons, said I fabricated the story because I didn't get the promotion I wanted."

"Were you looking for a higher position?"

"No. He was looking for a deputy chief of staff at the time, but I never applied nor had any interest in it, primarily because of the traveling involved. Washington is a detestable place to be."

I smiled. "We agree on that."

"It got worse. Kravitz spread all kinds of rumors, even

saying I had taken money from the petty cash account when he had personally instructed me to get five hundred dollars for him to drive up to Washington. It was awful. Some of the people I'd known for years looked at me differently. It really hurt."

"Sounds terrible. What happened next?"

"The congressional inquiry, if you could call it that, went nowhere. Kravitz tried to make me quit, but there was no way I was doing that. About three months after the inquiry fizzled out, he had Camber, his chief of staff, fire me. The coward didn't even have the nerve to do it himself. I started looking for a job and quickly realized Kravitz had blackballed me. Even Leahy, who recommended me for the position, said he couldn't take me back with all the rumors about my reputation."

"You couldn't find anything?"

"A master's in political science with a minor in marketing, and all I could get was a back-office position at City Furniture at less than half of what I was making."

"I don't usually get involved in political cases, but if I do, what would you like done?"

Ruta leaned in. "Kravitz has to be taken down. He's a monster. The more he gets away with the worse he'll become."

8

———

My foster bother, Mario, parked his Audi in my driveway. I hit the garage door opener. The closest thing I had to family bent down under the rising door. "Hey, man."

We hugged. I said, "Where is—"

"Left it in the car."

I kept my mouth shut as he clicked the pad, reversing the closing door. He grabbed a folder out of his car and shut the garage.

"You want something to drink?"

"Can you make a cup of coffee?"

"Sure." I put the Keurig on and took a dark-roast pod out of a drawer.

Mario opened the fridge and took out the skim milk. "How's it going with Laura?"

"Good."

"Things are getting serious, huh?"

"It's still early. How's Susan?"

"Good, but she's busting to have a baby."

"You sure you're ready for something like that?"

"I guess so."

"You can't guess with something like that. Besides, you should get married first."

"Plenty of people have kids without getting married."

I hit the brew button. "So what? It might be trendy, but it's not a good thing. Having a baby is a big responsibility."

As coffee filled a mug, he said, "I know it's a lot of work. You think you could do it?"

I shrugged. "I can't imagine having an infant. They're too delicate. And the diapers and being up all hours of the night. I think I would like to have kids, but it'd be nice to have one who comes out five years old."

I handed off the mug. Mario said, "Then you should adopt a kid."

"I don't have a problem with adoption, but I'd like to pass my genes on to someone."

Mario smiled. "You think you have special DNA or something?"

"Not really, but it'd be nice to keep my mom's lineage alive."

Mario's face darkened. "Not mine."

His mother was a crackhead. She had Mario while using, and he had to be weaned off drugs. "How's the coffee?"

"It's okay."

I sat across the kitchen table from him. "Let's get to work. What did you get on Simone Jackson?"

"Here's a picture of her."

Jackson was thin, with short brown hair. Forty-one years old, she had eyes as cold as a January morning in Maine.

Mario said, "She's been a social worker her entire career. Jackson has another three-plus years until retiring. With all the overtime she puts in, she's going to max out her benefits. She never takes any time off, no sick time, nothing."

"She might be hiding something by being at work all the time. She wants to control things."

"Maybe. Everybody said you don't want to cross her path because she'll come after you. She's a Nazi."

"That's the second time I heard someone call her that."

"Who else said that?"

"A lawyer who handled another case Jackson was involved in."

"If the shoe fits . . ."

"She have any family?"

"None I could find. She was born in Chicago, but I couldn't access her birth certificate. Illinois keeps them private, like Florida does. Jackson came here after graduating from Richard Daley Community College.

"Friends?"

"She's not that popular. Hangs a little with some coworkers, but she's basically a loner."

"Love life?"

He shook his head. "No significant other. Never married, no kids. But I got the names of two ex-boyfriends."

Mario gave the names and contact info, and I asked, "Hobbies?"

"She takes a walk most mornings, but other than gambling in casinos, it's work, work, work."

"Gambling? The slots?"

"No. She plays poker, Texas Hold'em."

"Unless you're very good, that's dangerous in a casino."

"Jackson's a regular at the Immokalee Casino and gets to the Hard Rock in Miami every couple of months."

"Interesting. Dig a little further into her family. I have a strong feeling there might be something there."

"I thought you didn't go by your gut. You said if you do the work you don't have to rely on instinct."

Few things were as annoying as having something you said thrown back in your face. "What do you think I've been doing? Sitting on my hands waiting for you?"

"Geez, you're sensitive." Mario shoved his chair back and stood. "I was just busting your balls, man."

"Where you going?"

"I got something to do."

The door slam confirmed he was mad. Whether it was with me or the fact that his mother was mentioned was up for grabs.

Digging out my cell, I called my lawyer friend, Larson. "Hey, Ray. You got a minute?"

"Sure. What can I assist with?"

"I need a little help digging further into Simone Jackson. She doesn't appear to have any family or friends outside of work, and I know you have contacts in the Windy City."

"She's from Chicago?"

"Yes. Jackson went to Richard Daley College."

"Good old Daley. He was the mayor of Chicago for over twenty years. He controlled everything, including the voting, some think. Many people believe JFK would never have won the presidency if it weren't for Daley."

"Years ago, I read a book, I think it was called *The Making of the President 1960*. It was written by someone close to him, a speechwriter, if I remember."

"Theodore White. He was a journalist and close to the campaign. Kennedy's father was instrumental, and Daley swung Illinois."

"They cheated, right?"

Larson snickered. "It's Chicago. So, when was Jackson in school?"

"She graduated in 1994, with an associate in social work. Can you find a way to locate a classmate she knew?"

"Shouldn't be a problem. Those are public records, but I have an old colleague of mine who works in the Cook County Clerk's office."

9

I CALLED THE THIRD NAME ON THE LIST LARSON HAD GIVEN ME. A woman answered, "Hello."

"Hi, is this Keisha Marrow?"

"Who's asking?"

"I'm a friend of Simone Jackson."

"I don't know anybody named that."

"You went to school with her in 1994."

"Thirty years ago?"

"Yes. She's a social worker too."

"I'm no social worker. I work for the city, the water department."

"Do you remember a Simone Jackson?"

"I told you, I don't know anyone like that. Now leave me alone."

She hung up.

There was one more name on the list, Lanny White. A smoker's voice answered, "Hello."

"Lanny White?"

"Yeah. What do you want?"

"I'm trying to track down someone you went to school with, Simone Jackson."

She hesitated. "Simone? I haven't seen her in, like, thirty years or something."

"You knew her?"

"Yeah, did something happen to her?"

"Yes, crazy as it seems, she got into an accident, and she's okay physically, but her memory is shot."

"Oh my God. What happened?"

"She was in a car crash and banged her head."

"You never know from one day to the next."

"That's so true. Look, the reason I'm calling is the doctors are saying we can help to jog her memory by reminding her of things in her past, especially when she was younger."

"I really didn't know her that well. We had two classes together."

"Anybody, say a teacher, stand out or something that happened?"

"Uh, I guess Mr. McMahon, he taught social psychology. He was good-looking, and we'd kid around about him, you know, like girls do."

"That's good info. Anything else? Any, like, events, like a concert you went to?"

"No. We didn't hang out much. It was a city college. We didn't live in a dorm or anything."

"How about her family? I can't seem to track anyone down."

"Simone didn't have any family. She told me she was abandoned and grew up in the foster care system."

I hesitated. "Oh no. That must have been terrible. Did you know who any of her foster parents were?"

"No. She didn't talk about it. She just said she was passed around a lot."

My stomach churned. "Sounds rough."

I finished the call and sent a text to Larson.

Construction on the uber-expensive Ritz Carlton Residences had begun. A hundred and twenty-eight multimillion-dollar apartments were slated to be occupied in 2025. Was there that much money sloshing around the nation?

I waved to Cabana Dan and headed to see Larson. Under a cloudless sky, Vanderbilt Beach was crowded. My confidant was on the phone, sitting on the edge of a chaise lounge in the shade. I lifted the lid of his cooler and grabbed a bottle of water.

A father was knee-deep in the water beckoning to his little boy. As soon as the water hit his ankles, the kid retreated. The father got out and picked the child up. He said something and took a couple of steps into the water.

A passing boat created a wave, and the boy wrapped his arms and legs around his dad. As Larson finished his call, the father lowered the boy into the water. He held his son's hands and pulled him along in the water. The smile on the boy's face made me grin.

Larson said, "God created the perfect playground."

"I remember going to the Jersey Shore with my mom when I was eight or so. My father wasn't into the beach, but Mom could stay all day."

"Good place to pile up the memories. Tommy practically grew up on Bonita Beach."

"Nice."

"Did the list help?"

"Yeah." I told him what I had learned about Jackson.

"No wonder she's so bitchy."

"I checked into Chicago's foster system. It's worse than

Jersey's by a long shot. CBS did a story recently on how many moves kids go through. One girl was in the system seventeen years and was moved sixty-seven times."

"That's outrageous. How can they expect her to live a normal life?"

"It's impossible. Believe me, Mario and I were moved three times, and it messes with your head. Some kids in Chicago were moved over a hundred times."

Larson wagged his head. "How the hell is that allowed?"

"Government may be well intentioned, but it sure as hell isn't accountable."

"And Jackson is on both sides of this."

"That's what makes it hard."

"It's natural to sympathize with her."

"I'm not sympathizing with her."

Larson looked me in the eye. "Okay."

"It just complicates things, you know?"

"Of course. But remember, you're trying to protect kids from being wrongfully stripped from their parents."

"And Jackson is just collateral damage?"

"Are you sure this isn't too close to home for you?"

"No, it's just . . ."

"It's difficult, but if you don't want to do it, don't. The ability to say no is more important than saying yes."

"I've gotten better at that."

"You have."

"On the way here, I was thinking Jackson got dealt a bad hand, you know?"

"She did, but so did you, Mario, and millions of others. I'm not discounting the impact of whatever happened to her, but keep in mind what Jackson did to the Dubers and who knows how many other families. It's just plain wrong."

"I wonder if Jackson is doing the crap she does as a twisted way to deny people what she never had."

"She may be vindictive, but it's best not to dwell on it. Keep your focus on preventing any other families from getting traumatized by her."

Larson was right, but he wasn't weighed down with the baggage I carried. "I'm going to make sure of that."

"Good. Are you working on a plan?"

"Been bouncing around a couple of ideas, but given everything, it's important to strike the right balance. I'm going to see what I can mine from a couple of her ex-boyfriends."

10

———————

Sitting on my lanai with my coffee, I scrolled through the *Naples Daily News*. On page five, a picture of a car crash at the Livingston Boulevard and Vanderbilt Beach intersection caught my attention.

It was the same location where my last big case began. This one also had a fatality. When I read the name, I sat back. Could it be the same Phil Tascon?

I Googled the name and the address of the deceased. It brought to mind Tascon's blue, Key West-styled home. He was my first client.

Tascon wanted to sue Robert McDuff, the owner of the construction site where his father died. His dad had fallen twelve stories, dying on impact.

No criminal charges were filed despite the fact that the City of Naples had fined Tascon's company six times in the past nine months over safety violations.

I was working for Larson at the time, and he asked me to look into the company and its practices. There was no doubt McDuff cut corners whenever possible, but he also had a written policy on working on an unenclosed building: anyone on the second floor or above had to wear a tethering device, unless fencing was installed.

Tascon's father had supposedly taken his tether off to take a leak. And when he slipped, he tumbled over the edge to his death.

If true, his father bore some responsibility for the accident, but countering it was anecdotal evidence that worker safety was a distant second to completion of a project.

After we investigated, Larson had Tascon come in to discuss the case. The three of us sat around a table in the conference room.

Tascon listened intently as we explained what we'd found. But he exploded when Larson said, "At the end of the day, my recommendation is we settle the case."

"Settle? What are you talking about? That bastard killed my father!"

"Take it easy. Law enforcement ruled your father's death to be accidental and—"

"But Beck said the bastard doesn't give a shit about his workers, all he worries about is the money."

Larson looked at me and I said, "It's really gray. I think McDuff plays it loose, at best. I tend to believe the rumors your father's tether was thrown down by McDuff or someone close to him."

Larson said, "The police investigation ruled that out."

"They did. I said I tend to believe it, but we have no proof."

"I can't believe this. He's going to get away with it?"

"We'll hit his pocketbook as deep as we can, but his resources are limited. He's still in debt from the hit real estate took during the financial crisis."

Tascon shook his head. "This is like losing Dad all over again."

"I'm sorry you feel that way. We did our best, but there's nothing criminal we can pin on him."

Tascon looked at me, saying, "What do you think? You know McDuff's a murderer, like I do."

I nodded. "But we're talking about being unable to prove it in a court of law."

"That's bullshit."

Larson said, "It's the reality we're working with. As a precursor to this meeting, I had a preliminary discussion with McDuff's lawyer, and it looks like they'd pay two hundred thousand to make this go away."

"So, that's what that bastard thinks my father's life is worth?"

"No, it's not like that at all."

"Yeah, right."

"Why don't you think it over, sleep on it, and we'll talk tomorrow."

Tascon shook his head and stormed out without saying a word.

A week later, I was leaving Larson's office and approaching my car when Tascon pulled up. He rolled his window down and said, "Hey, I need to talk to you."

"What about?"

"It won't take long. I'll meet you in the Rooms to Go parking lot, we can talk there."

Tascon didn't frighten me, but why the secrecy?

We parked in the rear of the building. I got out and leaned against my car. Tascon looked around as he approached.

"What's up?"

Tascon said, "Can I trust you?"

"Of course. Why are you asking that?"

"Whatever we talk about is between us, right?"

I nodded. "Are you going to tell me what's going on?"

Tascon lowered his voice. "I want you to kill McDuff."

"Excuse me?"

"You heard me. I want McDuff dead."

As I processed it, Tascon said, "Don't worry, I'll pay you to kill him."

"That's not the kind of work I do."

"It'll pay well. I'll give you the two hundred thousand settlement I'm getting."

"Like I said, I don't do that kind of thing."

"He lives in the middle of nowhere. You go after him at night, nobody will know."

"If it's so easy, why don't you do it?"

"I would, but the police would suspect me right off the bat."

"They probably would."

"Think about it. It's two hundred grand, and you'd be taking a scumbag out of the mix."

Before I could respond, Tascon walked back to his car. I stood in the parking lot for ten minutes mulling over what Tascon wanted.

I'd never killed before. I'd tried. I had set out to kill the foster father who'd abused me, but chickened out when I confronted him. I'd stabbed Mallory, but that was instinctual, punishing him for hitting me with a stick and not intending to kill him.

Realizing both incidents grew out of a need for revenge, I got back in my car and headed home. Two hundred thousand was hard to pass up. I was no assassin, but there had to be a way to help Tascon avenge his father's death and get paid for it.

11

———

LUNCH AT GROUPER AND CHIPS WAS ONE OF LIFE'S SMALL pleasures. I grabbed an outdoor table and bit into my broiled grouper sandwich. It hit the spot. Keeping my eyes on the corner where the hospital was, I popped a pan roll in my mouth.

I spied Ben Barnes crossing the street. His hair was whiter than his DMV photo. Stuffing the last of the grouper in my mouth, I got up and threw the Styrofoam clamshell in the trash.

"Ben? I'm Beck."

He extended his hand. "Hi."

"Hey, thanks for meeting me."

"No problem." He chuckled. "I eat here at least twice a week."

I circled back to my table. "You want something?"

"I'll grab an order of sweet potato fries when we're done."

"It's on me."

"That's not necessary."

"It's okay, I appreciate you making the time to talk to me about Simone Jackson."

"How is she doing?"

"Pretty good. I wanted to ask you about your time together. How long were you two a couple?"

"A little over a year. I should've bailed out earlier, but uh, I tried to make it work."

"You got along initially?"

"Yes. We had a couple of common interests."

"Such as?"

"Well, I liked to go to the casinos, you know, gamble a little, maybe see a show, but nothing like Simone; she could park herself at a table and play for hours."

"Was that the issue that got in the way?"

"No, not really. I don't want to make her look like a monster or something, but she was cold, you know, emotionless. It bothered me, but I thought the ice would melt the longer we stayed together."

"It didn't?"

He wagged his head. "I couldn't take it anymore. Don't get me wrong, I'm no mush bag, but my mother was dying, and Mom and I were really close. I was a basket case, but Simone didn't seem to understand how much it hurt. When Mom went into hospice, Simone acted like it was nothing. Right there and then, I ended it. It was crazy, you know?"

"I'm sorry, it must have been hard on you."

"It was. Mom has been gone two years, and I still can't believe it."

"I know what you mean. Mine died when I was ten, and uh, well, it sucks." I took a sip of my iced tea. "Is there anything else you can tell me about her?"

"What are you investigating? Is she in trouble?"

"I don't know, the law firm I work for just asked for background on her."

"Okay. Look, Simone's not a bad person, but she's not for me."

"Thanks. Let's get you those fries."

It was a short drive to see another man Jackson dated. Scott Palmer was an auto mechanic at the Valvoline Oil shop on Golden Gate Parkway.

Palmer asked me to text him, and I did. He came out of the garage, and I waved him over.

"Thanks for meeting me. I promise to be quick. As I said, I'm an investigator for a law firm and they need background on Jackson. What can you tell me about her since you dated her?"

"She in some kind of jam?"

"I don't know, but it's nothing criminal or anything like that. We don't handle those types of cases. How long did you go out with her?"

"Around eight months. Don't get me wrong, we had some fun, but she's weird. I mean, let's say Simone is, like, distant, you know?"

"She doesn't let you in?"

"Yeah, like there's a wall around her or something."

"She ever talk about her family?"

"Never. I asked her a couple of times, but she'd say she wasn't close with them and that was it. I didn't press it because she seemed to thrive on conflict."

"I've heard she likes to gamble."

"She does, and I like to too, but not as much as she does. And she bets a lot. One night she was losing over a thousand at the Immokalee Casino, and I told her it was time to go home. But she didn't want to leave. I ended up in the lounge watching a guy play the piano, for like, two hours."

"Was it the gambling that broke you guys up?"

"Not really. It was a couple of things. I've got two kids with my ex, and Simone didn't even want to meet them. I mean, we were going out for several months. It ended up being for the best anyway."

"Anything else you can tell me?"

He shrugged. "It may sound silly, but I was turning forty and I wanted to go somewhere to celebrate. Nowhere crazy. I suggested we go the Keys for the weekend, but she nixed it, saying it was stupid making a big deal over a birthday."

I thanked him for his time and left. Driving home, I rolled around the ideas I had for getting back at Simone. My ideas had evolved since my first case, where planting bones and Indian artifacts on McDuff's construction site had shut down construction for eight months. Tascom wanted McDuff dead, but shutting down the business led to his bankruptcy.

Tascom didn't get what he wanted, but he was pleased to put McDuff out of business. The success and money he paid, launched me into a business that had more cases than I could handle.

12

STEPPING ONTO THE SAND, A THIN CLOUD COVER TOOK THE edge off the shadows. Vanderbilt Beach was busy for a Tuesday. My lawyer-confidant Larson was undercover at his usual slice of beach next to the Ritz Carlton Resort.

"What are you reading?"

Larson put down a thick book. "*The Splendid and the Vile.* It's about Churchill and what happened right before America got into the Second World War."

"He was a giant."

"In my opinion, the defining influence in the last hundred years."

"Is it true he would parade around naked?"

"Yes. It's that genius-madness thing."

I took a water bottle out of his cooler. "You see it all over."

A boat loaded with parasailers pulled away from the shore. Larson pointed. "You ever go up in one of those?"

"No way. Me and heights don't get along."

"You'd be amazed how serene it is when you're way up there."

"So, what do you have for me?"

"A new case. Have you heard of Gordon Whitmore?"

"Sounds familiar, but I can't place him."

"South Florida Aeronautics."

"Oh yeah, the company that went public in that reverse merger thing and then went bankrupt."

"That's it. They were a family business for almost forty years. Whitmore really built it up, but going to the next level, competing against the Boeings and McDonnell Douglases of the world, pushed him into the public markets."

"Weren't they supposed to have a deal with SpaceX?"

"I don't recall all the facts, but that was definitely in the air."

"What's the reason you're telling me all this?"

"Whitmore is old school. He's a good man, but he may have made a mistake listening to consultants about going private. He's stressed out. When everything collapsed, he had to lay off close to two thousand people. Whitmore insists business was good, but that rumors and short sellers forced him to go bust."

"He lost it all?"

"His family had a ton of stock, so he took a major hit, but he probably squirreled away enough over the years to be comfortable."

"You mentioned a short seller? What's that?"

"Most people invest in the stock market hoping a stock goes up, and when it does, they make money. That's called being 'long a stock.' But you can also make money when a stock goes down if you bet against it. The people who do that are called short sellers."

"How do they do that?"

"They borrow shares from a broker. If the price goes down, they buy it back at the lower price and pocket the difference. Say company A's stock is a hundred a share today. They sell it at a hundred, and if it drops to eighty, they buy it back to replace what they got at a hundred and make twenty dollars a share."

"What happens if it goes up, say, to a hundred and ten?"

"They lose ten dollars a share."

"So you can bet a stock goes down and win. Kind of like the Don't Pass Line in craps where you hope the person throwing the dice doesn't win?"

He winced. "Perhaps, in a broad sense. The simple way to think of it is, you're betting the stock goes down when most people hope it goes up."

"Contrarian, then."

"It's more complicated than that. Sometimes, people believe a stock got ahead of itself, you know, it ran up too high, and other times they believe macro events, like new technology, will make a product or business obsolete."

"Is it riskier than hoping a stock goes up?"

"Yes. If you're long a stock, hoping it goes up, and it goes down or stays the same, you don't have to do anything. But if you short a stock and it goes up, the opposite of what you want it to do, you'll have to come up with more money to support your position."

"And if you don't have the dough?"

"You have to liquidate the position and take the loss."

"It sounds convoluted. So, what does this have to do with Whitmore?"

"It's better you go see him. He can fill you in."

I frowned.

"You'll like him, he's a regular guy."

I slid onto a chair at the last empty table at Joe's Diner. Their breakfast menu paid homage to what was once America's sport:

baseball. As Mario walked up, I decided to go for the Yogi Berra.

"Hey." We fist-bumped.

My step-brother said, "I need coffee, bad."

"Here she comes."

The server poured two cups of steaming java. "You boys know what you want?"

"I'm having the Yogi."

"Well, since you're here, I'm going with the Babe." He smiled. She didn't return it and walked away.

I picked up my mug. "Thrown out trying to steal."

"Ha-ha. Very funny. She's hot."

"What are you flirting for? Things good with Susan?"

"Yeah, just playing around. A little harmless fun."

Mario sipped his coffee. His eyes were bloodshot.

I said, "Look, this child protection case is something we're probably going to do."

He arched an eyebrow. "All right. How much is it paying?"

"It's going to be freebie."

"What? That's not—"

"You'll get paid. Don't worry."

"I'm not worried. It's just stupid."

"These people got screwed and have no money. In fact, the whole thing put them forty grand in the hole, paying for lawyers."

"You know, you can't save the world."

"I'm not trying to."

He rolled his red eyes. Was he smoking weed in the morning?

The server swooped in, setting our platters down. "Enjoy."

Mario used a fork to cut a piece. "Looks good."

I swallowed a bite. "It is."

"What do you want me to cover on this?"

"There's a doctor, Narid Khan, who might be green-lighting whatever Simone Jackson, the woman who runs a lot of these cases, wants. Check him out, see if there is any connection to Jackson."

"No problem."

"He's at the Physician's Regional Hospital on Collier Boulevard."

13

———

Turning off Mooring Line Drive, I made a right onto Bow Line Drive. Gordon Whitmore's home wasn't on the bay, and it hadn't been rebuilt like most of the others in the neighborhood.

Nestled between a pair of houses, too big for their lots, stood Whitmore's one-story home. According to tax records, he'd owned the place for thirty-four years.

Two giant oak trees shaded the front yard. I rang the bell.

Silver hair receding, Whitmore had a sparkle in his eyes. "Mr. Beck, please come in."

The house was dark but comfortable. Whitmore took a seat in a brown recliner. "Peggy's out with one of our daughters, so we can talk freely."

"Perfect. Mr. Larson provided a bit of background, but I'd appreciate hearing everything that happened from you."

"Sure. Say, can I get you anything?"

"No, thanks."

"All right. Well, my dad started what became South Florida Aeronautics in the late fifties, when air travel started taking off. It was a small business, but it grew over the years. Not to take away from what Dad did, but it's easier to make a business work if the industry you're in is booming." He pointed at me. "It's good to keep that in mind if you ever venture into business."

"I appreciate that. It's solid advice."

"After I graduated from FSU, I joined the company, and my role expanded over the years. The business had basically become a subcontractor for McDonnell Douglas, and being reliant on one company made me uncomfortable." He looked me in the eye. "You have to control your destiny as best as possible."

"More good counsel."

He smiled. "I finally took over the reins in the mid-nineties and focused on building the relationship we had with what's now called Northrop Grumman. They had a sizable contract with NASA, and it was growing fast."

Whitmore was one of the few who took his own advice.

"Working on spaceships must be complicated."

He shrugged. "I like to say more complex. There's a lot of components to making a product for space, but that doesn't necessarily make it difficult."

That needed thinking over. "Please continue."

"We created a division to focus on the satellite end of things. It took off like we never could have imagined."

"Good call by you."

"It was a team effort, but one thing I didn't foresee was how much capital was needed to get to the next level. I mean, we had a good, moneymaking business. I made more than I ever dreamed of, but just to maintain what we had, we had to invest in all kinds of high-tech machinery and software." He sighed. "It's one thing to build an airplane and a completely other thing to build a spacecraft that can make it to outer space or do what Musk is doing with reusable rockets."

"SpaceX is doing fascinating things."

"It is. Proves private enterprise can run circles around the government, no matter how much money the politicians throw at it."

"You worked with SpaceX?"

"The field was exploding, and SpaceX and a couple of others in the field needed reliable partners to supply them. I knew we could do it if we had the resources. So, we talked to a couple of investment bankers about raising the money to build two new facilities. They said the two billion or so needed was impossible to raise privately. They suggested going public." He scoffed, "You know what they actually said? They said the private markets would only pay a certain multiple of earnings, but the public would pay a hundred times what we were making."

"That says a lot about how they view the public markets."

"It sure does, but they were right, to a degree. They said the easiest way to go public was to do a reverse merger into an already existing entity. You ever hear of what they call a SPAC?"

"Not really."

"It stands for Special Purpose Acquisition Company. It's a company with no operations. Its sole purpose is to raise capital through an IPO, an initial public offering. Once they're public and have the money, they merge with an existing company like ours."

"Sounds kind of crazy."

"I thought so too, but that Brit, Richard Branson, his Virgin Galactic did it that way. It made it seem more legitimate, if you know what I mean."

"I get it. So, what happened?"

"A lot of things. We broke ground and things were going pretty well, and then, you know, costs started skyrocketing.

Some of it was the technology needed, some was mission creep, but a lot was inflation. Our labor costs went up over fifty percent. It was one thing after another. Our bankers said we could get a billion-dollar credit line from JP Morgan. It sounded good, but it got us in deeper trouble."

"You couldn't pay it back?"

"We actually were current, but there was a covenant in the loan documentation that gave us a major problem. When we started drawing the money down, our stock was fifty-one dollars a share. The clause said if our stock went below thirty-five, they could call the loan.

"Make you pay it back?"

"Yes. Covid hit, and we took a beating like everybody else did. But our stock held up okay; it was in the low forties. Then that bastard Melvin Weiss started the rumor mills." He pounded his fist on his thigh.

"What did he spread?"

"Lies. One after another. He and his bullshit company, Chernobyl. I mean, who the hell names a company after a disaster?"

It was a valid point. It may have been a marketing ploy. "It is weird. What did they say?"

"The biggest thing was the report they published saying SpaceX would never do business with us and that Musk wanted everything in-house. It was completely fabricated. We'd had a meeting with his top lieutenants the week before. We put a press release out, and then Weiss sensationalized a fire we had in our Cape Canaveral facility. It was mostly contained in the maintenance area, but Weiss said the factory was destroyed and it would take a year-plus to rebuild. It was utter nonsense."

"That's terrible."

"Oh, it didn't stop there. Out of nowhere there was an effort to unionize the plants. I couldn't believe it. We're a tight-knit outfit; we take care of our people, and they know it. We did some research, and I'm convinced Weiss was behind it."

"How so?"

"He had connections with a union and made a contribution to them. They had no shot of getting our people to vote yes, but the uncertainty took a bite out of our stock price."

"Sounds frustrating."

"It was, and every little thing, you know, normal staff turnover was blown out of proportion. This one guy, who'd been with us a decade—he was an assistant to our director of material procurement—he took a job in Texas, and Weiss made it look like people were leaving. He had the gall to say our people were jumping off a sinking ship."

"I'm guessing this impacted the stock."

"Of course. We dropped to a low of twenty-two before bouncing, as Weiss said on CNBC, like a dead cat, to twenty-six and a half."

"That's terrible."

"I went on CNBC, using Zoom, as soon as I could. I defended the company, but Weiss was in the studio, and he kept shaking his head. The bastard said people should bail out of our stock, that if there was smoke it meant there was a fire, and we were going to zero. Zero. I had our CFO release what he could under SEC guidelines to prove that we weren't in trouble. But the press kept touting Weiss and his long record of predicting business failures." He wagged his head. "Now, I know how he did it."

"Did JP Morgan call the loan?"

"At the speed of light. To stay afloat, I had to cut expenses. The hardest thing I ever did was laying off two thousand of our hard-working employees. Outside of the stupid lockdowns, in over sixty years, even through the financial crisis, we never laid off a soul."

"Are you personally okay, financially speaking?"

"Yes. I lost ninety percent of my wealth, but me and my family are fine, unlike the others who lost their livelihoods. I helped a lot of them, but too many lost their houses and cars. But I'm okay, and I have no problem paying the fee Mr. Larson mentioned."

I nodded. "If I take this on, what would you like me to do?"

Whitmore leaned forward. "Make sure that bastard, Weiss, doesn't do this to anybody else. All he cares about is money. He's got to be stopped before he ruins more lives."

14

I SAT AT A TABLE AT THE END OF DOLCE AND SALATO'S terrace. The Italian eatery closed at 3 p.m., and the remaining diners were lingering over cups of expresso.

We were meeting for coffee, but the smells had me waving down a server. I ordered a prosciutto cotto as a man I recognized from a picture as Barney Fitzgerald, strolled onto the deck. I stood and we shook hands.

"I'm glad you suggested this place."

Fitzgerald's face was red. Not from the sun but from drinking. "Oh, it's great. I couldn't resist ordering a prosciutto sandwich. You want something to eat?"

"No, I had a seven a.m. tee off and ate an early lunch. But I'll grab a sfogliatella for my wife on the way out."

"One of my favorites. You should put the order in when he comes back. They like to get out of here at three on the button."

He smiled. "We know. They're real Italians."

"Anyway, uh, thanks for meeting with me."

"Sure. Anything for Gordon."

"You get along with Mr. Whitmore?"

"Sure. I mean, we've had some disagreements, but Gordon is a salt-of-the-earth kind of guy."

"You were second in command?"

"No. But let's say I was a trusted lieutenant."

"What can you tell me about him and the business?"

"There's a lot there. I wouldn't know where to start."

"How about when things started going bad, you know, with the SpaceX thing and short sellers attacking the company. How did Whitmore react?"

"He's a tough SOB. You know, one of those old-time guys who isn't afraid of knocking his head against the wall believing he'd eventually make a crack."

"Sounds like he was stubborn."

"Sure, but it was a good thing. I mean, if he believed in something, he'd see through it to the end."

"But that brings trouble, like the foray into supersonic jets."

"It did. We poured a ton of money into it, but you know, I think we were just ahead of the times."

The server set down a work of art. Paper-thin slices of prosciutto were hanging out between two slices of fresh bread.

"Can I get you something?"

Fitzgerald ordered a double expresso and the pastry for his wife.

"Go ahead and eat."

"It's okay. I want to keep talking. You mentioned Whitmore being stubborn."

"Persistent is the way I like to think of it."

"Fair enough. But it did get the company in trouble."

"Yes and no. I mean, we didn't have the cash to withstand what came next with the fire and the lies about us. But who could've predicted that?"

I smelled the Italian coffee before it was set down.

"I'm not here to criticize Mr. Whitmore, but did his

management . . . shall we say, style, add to the company's problems?"

"Gordon did the best he knew how. I mean, we could've used one of those Fortune 500 guys, but what would we have lost? And you think any of those bums would've dug into their own pockets when things got ugly?"

"Whitmore put his own money in when things got tough?"

"Oh yeah. I think he put ten million in to prevent layoffs. Unfortunately, they ended up losing their jobs because that bastard Weiss kept spreading his lies."

"That's a lot of money."

"Whitmore is one of the best people I've ever had the privilege of knowing."

"How confident are you that if Weiss hadn't done what he did, that the company would've been okay?"

"There's not a shred of doubt in my mind. We had some issues to deal with, but they were very manageable. Weiss should be behind bars for destroying so many lives."

15

I'D PASSED MELVIN WEISS'S HICKORY BOULEVARD HOME countless times, assuming the ocean-front structure housed a couple of condos. Scooping up my laptop and recorder, I got out. The breeze was warm and salt infused.

A woman in a uniform opened the door. Behind her, the Gulf of Mexico merged into an infinity pool. "Mr. Beck?"

"Yes."

"Please come in. Mr. Weiss is on the lanai."

The floor of the main area was hockey-rink white. A rose-colored grand piano anchored the space. Large pieces of modern art occupied the limited wall space the home had.

We passed a sweeping staircase leading to another level and stepped onto an expanse that defied description as a lanai. Three seating areas and a King Arthur-length dining table balanced a beckoning pool.

The lord of the mansion was seated to the left.

Weiss put down an iPad and tapped his oversized wrist-watch. "Right on time. Timing is everything in life."

His teeth were like Chiclets. "Doing the number of interviews I do, you have to be punctual."

"My mother taught me to respect everyone's time. She used to say we only have so much of it. And you don't know when it's going to run out."

Nodding, my gaze settled on a sculpture, a recognizable, stainless-steel shape. "That's an unusual piece."

"It's the mushroom cloud from a nuclear explosion."

"Chernobyl?"

"They didn't have an explosion. That was a man-made disaster. A quite predictable one. I saw it coming when I started my business and shorted utilities around the world." He rubbed his forefinger and thumb together. "Made a killing and decided to name my company Chernobyl Investments."

"Nuclear is safe, isn't it?"

"It's the way to go. The Russians—Soviets they were called at the time—didn't have our safety standards and still don't. We overengineer like mad, and with the technological advances over the last thirty years, nuclear is predictable, cheap, and the safest source of energy we have."

"It's out of favor though."

"It shouldn't be. Wait until everybody's electric bills skyrocket. Look what happened in Europe. Nuclear needs to be in the mix, or prices are going up on everything."

"Solar and wind aren't going to cut it?"

Weiss scoffed. "They can help, but you want to know something off the record?"

"Sure."

"Most of these green companies aren't going to make it. If you own them, get out. But make sure that isn't in your article."

"No problem, sir."

"Mel, call me Mel."

The lady who greeted me came onto the lanai with a tray. She poured two glasses of iced tea and set them on the cocktail table.

"Thank you, Rosa. Could you put the screens down? The glare is a bit too much."

"Yes, sir."

A low hum sounded as white screens lowered. The glare was gone but not the Gulf of Mexico. Weiss checked his watch. "Shall we get started?"

"Sure. Is it okay to record this?"

"Go for it."

I clicked the recorder on. "I wanted to thank you for agreeing to be interviewed by *Wired Magazine*."

"It's my pleasure. Your outfit is one of the few publications to survive the move to digital. I made a few dollars betting against the likes of *Life* and *Consumers Digest*. It was easy pickings. Who needs a magazine with pictures or one about products when there are millions of images and reviews online?"

I poured two packets of sweetener in my glass and took a sip. "Good question, and perfect segue. How did you see that coming when so many others failed to?"

"Coke doesn't reveal it's secret ingredients, do they?"

I drew a circle on the condensation forming on my glass. "No. But each situation you invest in is different. What can you tell us about the principles that guide you?"

He pointed a finger at me. "That's an excellent way to frame it. And very insightful of you. As you say, every decision to invest, or frankly, not put my money in, differs in many ways, but usually there is a commonality."

"I'm on the edge of my seat."

"Sit back. Melvin looks at how a business is being managed. Poorly? Is their business model outdated? Like the magazines we spoke about. Or is an emerging technology about to disrupt an industry? Also, the simple fact is, it's getting increasingly difficult for medium-sized businesses to make it.

Mom-and-pops will always be around, but middle-market companies are inundated with regulations and face larger, better-positioned competitors with the resources to sway politicians."

Did he refer to himself in the third person? I took a gulp of iced tea and asked, "And when you identify one that fits a criterion, you short it?"

"If Melvin believes the timing is right, yes."

"Why did you decide to focus on the short side rather than the long side?"

"Another good question. Frankly, there's less competition. There are hedge funds who go long and short but not many pure short players in the marketplace."

"Why do you believe short sellers are looked at differently than those who bet a company will go higher?"

"It's the American psyche. Americans are an optimistic people. Not as much as we used to be, but we largely believe in positive outcomes. Short selling goes against that core belief."

"Do you get a lot of hate mail?"

Weiss laughed. "At times, I do."

"Considering the layoffs at some of the companies you've shorted, do you think it's justified?"

Weiss leaned forward. "Look, what I do is force these companies to face reality. People may lose their jobs as a firm makes adjustments to cut costs to stay in business, but the fact is, I'm saving jobs. If they didn't adapt, the company would go out of business, and everybody would be out on the street."

He shifted back to first person. "So, you consider what you do a service to the company and its employees?"

"Melvin realizes it's tough for most people to understand, but he simply accelerates what is going to happen. When we short a company, we force them to act. They can take action, or they can bleed a slow death into oblivion."

"The macro-opportunities are easy to understand, like seeing what Artificial Intelligence is going to do to certain businesses. But you've targeted companies who seem to be doing well, claiming their financials aren't what they appear to be. How do you get that information?"

"We piece it together. We talk to a lot of people, employees, suppliers, and competitors to get a more rounded view than what the executives tell the public."

"Anecdotal information?"

"At times."

"Can't that be misinterpreted or wrong?"

"Sometimes it can be."

"What if someone has an agenda, wants to cause trouble for a company?"

"We don't look at just one data point."

"Fair enough. You received some bad press in Southwest Florida regarding South Florida Aeronautics. Gordon Whitmore is a local legend."

"Local is the right descriptor. Look, he may be a nice man and all, but Whitmore is used to hitting off a tee, and making the jump to the big leagues was a helluva a lot harder than he supposed."

"I don't know all the ins and outs, but he had a successful business, and everything was going well until the rumors started circulating that things weren't as good as they seemed."

"They weren't, and it was proven to be true."

"But from what I read, and I haven't read everything, there was nothing behind—"

"Earlier you asked about process, well the time to act is when you first smell smoke. If you wait until someone is yelling there's a fire, you're too late."

The slider opened and Rosa stepped out. "Excuse me, sir.

The missus asked me to remind you that you're due at the club in thirty minutes."

"Thank you, Rosa. We're going to have to wrap this up. My wife is running an event for Youth Haven and wants me there. She does a lot of great work in the community, and I consider it my duty to support her."

"I understand. I hear they're a good organization."

"They are. My wife, Cynthia, is on the board, and we're hosting a party for friends and donors on Saturday afternoon."

"That's nice of her to give back."

"She's a great woman."

"How long are you married?"

"Closing in on forty years."

"Wow. What's the secret?"

He pointed at the recorder. I shut it off.

"I got lucky with Cynthia. Without her, I don't know where'd I be. When you do get married, you're got to work at it. We've been married thirty-eight-years, and I can tell you the biggest thing I've learned is not to disappoint my wife."

"That's good advice. I've had a difficult time settling down, you know, making a commitment to one woman."

Weiss leaned forward, lowering his voice. "You can play around, just don't make it more than that, and make sure the wife doesn't find out."

I smiled. "You make it sound so easy."

He shrugged. "Her charitable work and obsession with all things equestrian provide plenty of opportunity."

"Cynthia is into horseback riding?"

"That's putting it mildly. We have a ranch in Ocala, and when she goes there, I have time for my hobby." He smiled and said, "I'm sorry, but I've got to go."

I stood. "That's okay. I think I have enough. If not, I'll make another appointment."

"Sounds good."

"Do you mind if I use your restroom on the way out?"

He extended his hand. "The powder room is on your left, opposite the dining room. It was nice meeting you."

I shook his manicured hand. "Same here, sir. You gave me a lot to think about."

I slipped into the bathroom. A sink was sunk into a block of marble Michelangelo would love to get his hands on. An expensive piece of modern art was hung over the toilet. I used my phone and snapped a dozen pictures.

16

Sitting at an outdoor table at True Food, I marveled at how crowded Waterside Shops was. Filled with high-end retailers, the mall seemed recession proof. Naples was in a bubble, but it wasn't going to burst.

Frank Locastro weaved through the tables. "Sorry, I got hung up on a call with a client."

"No problem. Are you staying busy at Morgan Stanley?"

"Oh, definitely. A lot of people are worried the market is too high, and now with interest rates so high, there's a lot of people that want to stay in cash."

"After years of getting nothing, savers are finally getting something."

"Yes and no. Don't forget, if the banks are paying you five percent, inflation is higher than that. Bottom line is, you're still falling behind."

"Figures." I picked up a menu. "I like the Ancient Grain bowl."

"That's what I always get."

We put our orders in, and I said, "Tell me the good side of shorting a stock."

"You don't want to play in that arena, Beck."

"It's not something I'm looking to do. There's a case I'm considering taking on, and I need to understand all the angles. So, what's the good side of it?"

"Short selling plays an important role in the efficiency of markets. It facilitates secondary markets, improves price discovery, and impacts corporate governance."

"Price discovery?"

"The price of a stock. We've seen it over and over, like the rush to green energy and electric vehicles, in particular. People pile into them, but outside of Telsa, nobody is close to making money. These companies are trading at unrealistic valuations, burning through cash, and short sellers can have an effect to bring them down to reality."

"By pointing out how they'll never make the kind of money to support the stock price?"

"In a roundabout way, yes."

"And the corporate governance thing. Explain that."

"Well, when a company's stock price is high, it can mask the underlying situation. There's no pressure on management to do anything to fix a business's problems. When the shorts attack, management is forced to take action."

The server set our bowls down. Frank said, "If you would have told me I'd be eating this twenty years ago, I would've told you you were crazy."

I scooped up a forkful of quinoa. "Same here. But it's good."

As Frank dug in, I said, "So short sellers have a role?"

"Yes. They get a lot of bad press, but the good ones serve a purpose. They do deep dives on companies, and the research is invaluable."

"Who are the good ones?"

"John Paulson, he made twenty billion when he saw the

mortgage market for what it was in 2008. Jim Chanos is also good, along with Ackman and Livermore."

"Where does Melvin Weiss fit in?"

The eye roll was telling. "He's done well, but what he did with South Florida Aeronautics didn't pass the smell test."

"I heard he was lying."

"The company had its trouble, but I read the research report Morgan Stanley put out. I'm no analyst, but their financial situation wasn't that bad."

"Can you send that to me?"

I signed in to my VPN and searched Gulf Shore Life's website for pictures of the Naples charity scene. Toby curled up beside my chair. Short seller Weiss and his wife appeared in pictures of four of last month's events.

Toby's stomach made a weird sound. "You okay, boy?"

He pulled into a tighter circle. It'd been a month since he'd kept me up all night. He hadn't relieved himself on our normal six o'clock walk. I'd take him out again before going to bed.

Split screening my monitor, I pulled up Youth Haven's website and compared the ladies on their board to those on Gulf Shore Life's pictures. There were three matches. I copied the images and jotted down the names.

Checking further into Weiss's wife, I discovered both he and she were on the boards of the Guadalupe Center and the Baker Senior Center. The Bakers, whose name was plastered all over Naples, led the town's philanthropic crowd.

I navigated to the Guadalupe Center's website. Their home page advertised a gala event named A Night in Morocco. The annual affair was the flagship fundraiser for the charity. It wasn't surprising to see the names of Cynthia and Melvin Weiss listed as co-chairs.

Weiss seemed nice enough, but it was certain his wife was the one spearheading their giving. The short seller was rumored to be worth close to six hundred million dollars. Collecting more money was behind climbing the social and personal recognition ladder.

About to do another search, Toby's stomach creaked. I pushed away from the desk. "Come on, boy. We're going for a walk."

I put his leash on, and we stepped outside.

A dark sedan crawled down the street. It was the only car. Toby pulled me toward a mailbox. He did his business, I bagged it, hoping his action would calm his stomach, and we headed back.

The rear lights of the car disappeared around the corner. Approaching my driveway, a rustling in the bushes between the house next door caught my attention. I stopped, studying the pitch-black area.

Toby started barking. I took a step toward the green alley-way, and a figure dressed in black bolted away. I started after him with Toby. He was carrying something.

Was it a gun?

I stopped, and the man ran left onto the golf course and into the darkness. Who was he and what was he doing here? After notifying the security patrol, I retreated inside.

As Toby chewed his Greenies dental treat, I alarmed the house and made sure the doors were locked. I called the guard at the gatehouse: no one had entered or left in the last two hours at either entrance.

It was surprising. If a pro wanted to get in a gated community, the security theater wouldn't deter them. The question was whether I'd been targeted, and if so, by whom?

17

———

MARIO BREEZED INTO RUSTY'S OUTDOOR BAR AREA. HE FIT right in, wearing cargo shorts and a beaded necklace. He flashed a thumbs-up and headed to the high-top I was perched at.

He slid onto a chair. "Hey."

Fist-bumping, I detected the acrid smell of marijuana. Was smoking weed the reason he was always relaxed? He seemed to have shaken off our foster-family experience.

The only time I'd seen Mario get angry was when we hunted down the foster father who beat us regularly. When the opportunity to push the drunk bastard into the roiling Atlantic Ocean went down the tubes, he morphed into an angry monster I didn't recognize.

I sniffed. "You just smoke a joint?"

"Yeah, why?"

"Don't overdo that crap."

He smiled, pointing at my glass of vodka. "Don't overdo the Tito's, daddy."

I frowned. "At least I know what's in a bottle. You have no

idea what they're putting in the stuff you buy. Some dealers are putting fentanyl in everything."

"You're always worrying. You have to chill out, man."

Easier said than done.

A ponytailed server came over. "What can I get you?"

Mario answered, "A bottle of Heineken."

"Anything to eat?"

I said, "You want to split a platter of BLT sliders?"

"Yeah, they're good."

The server promised to add another slider to the three the dish came with and left.

Lowering my voice, I asked, "What did you find out about the doctor?"

Mario stuck a finger up. The server appeared, setting Mario's bottle of beer down before leaving.

"He's got the backbone of a snake." Mario took a swig and continued, "Khan seems like a nice enough guy, but he goes with the flow."

"That's because he's new and not from the States."

"It goes deeper than that."

I swirled my vodka with the straw instead of saying something about having to pull information out of him. "In what way?"

"Here you go, guys. Enjoy." The server set down our BLTs and a roll of paper towels.

Mario picked up a slider and took a bite. "Man, this is good. The only problem is they're too small." He laughed.

"What about Khan?"

"Guess who sponsored him on the visa application?"

"The hospital?"

"Nope." He stuffed the rest of the slider in his mouth.

I counted to ten as he wiped his mouth. "Who got Khan in the country?"

"Simone Jackson."

"Are you shitting me?"

He reached for another slider. "Nope. Khan told me a friend of his father's works at Physician Regional, and they don't get involved with the whole visa-green card thing anymore because it was costing them too much for immigration attorneys. Anyway, this guy is friends with Jackson. He told Simone about Khan and that the hospital would hire him if he could get into the country. Jackson went ahead and sponsored him."

"And now Khan owes her."

"No doubt."

"What kind of experience does he have with caring for infants?"

"None that I could find. Kahn is a regular, you know, general practice-type doctor. He's been there just a couple of years."

"Shit. He probably just started when the Duber kid was brought in. There was no way he was going to buck what Jackson wanted."

"Probably not."

"He say anything about her?"

"Kahn said Jackson is always checking on him; she doesn't trust him. Oh yeah, listen to this—he said she wouldn't approve his vacation to go see his parents in India. Even though he had three weeks coming to him, she made him take the trip in just a week. He wanted to go to HR but was afraid of her getting retribution."

"That's nuts to go that far for a week. I mean, the flight is twenty-hours long. You basically burn two days traveling back and forth."

"This woman sounds like a bully, and we know the type, don't we?"

An image of the last foster father Mario and I had flooded

my head. "It's all about insecurity. That jerkoff Bryant pushed us around to make himself feel good."

"We should have done him in when we had the chance."

"It doesn't matter; he's dead now."

"Well, it goddamn matters to me!" He slid off the chair. "We done? I have to get moving. I'm getting new tires put on the chariot."

"Sure. I got the bill. We'll talk later."

The anger surprised me. Mario wasn't as easygoing as he wanted you to believe, or was something bothering him? I threw a fifty on the table, waved to the bartender, and hustled after Mario.

He was backing out of a space near Pet Oasis Animal Hospital. I knocked on the side of the car and he hit the brakes.

"What's the matter?"

The car was hot. "I forgot to mention, the other night I was walking Toby. It was later than usual, and on the way back I saw a man hiding by the side of my house."

"Who was it?"

"I don't know. Have you noticed anything weird? Anything suspicious?"

"No. Nothing."

"Okay. Keep your eyes open."

"It was probably nothing."

"Hiding behind my bushes at ten at night?"

"It could have been a thief. Doesn't mean he was targeting you."

"Maybe. But either way, stay alert."

Mario smiled. "Don't worry, Nervous Nellie."

I squeezed into a spot along Cape Hickory Court. The dead-end street was lined with the cars of beachgoers. Diagonally across traffic-packed Hickory Boulevard was the mansion I'd been to. A pair of valets were setting up in the driveway of the Weiss home.

Window lowered, I leaned out, zoomed my camera in, and snapped several pictures of the couple getting out of a blue Bentley. The woman, in a white dress that hugged her curves, looked familiar.

Before they hit the stairs, a silver Aston Martin pulled up. A younger woman, wearing white jeans and a red top, handed her keys to the valet. She and her passenger, a thin, gray-haired lady with a marine's posture, waited for a Mercedes to pull up behind them.

I took a dozen photos, mostly of the older ladies, as a line of cars formed to get to the charity event. It was barely a minute before the affair's starting time. Were they respecting Weiss's penchant for being on time?

After taking pictures of a half a dozen other attendees, I left, satisfied I had ammo if Weiss had not played fair.

18

———

AS THE CHEERING FROM A CRAPS TABLE DIED DOWN, A YOUNG man took a seat next to Simone Jackson at a poker table. The dealer dealt each player at the table two hole cards. Everyone looked at their cards, and the first player tossed a green chip into the center.

The second player raised him, throwing two chips in. The next player folded, pushing his cards toward the dealer.

Simone Jackson was seated last. As the young man next to her matched the bet, she took another peek at her cards. Following the man, she also shoved a pair of chips into the pot.

The dealer laid out five community cards, facedown. He quickly scanned the players and turned over the flop cards. The first card was a king of diamonds, the second an eight of clubs, and the third a jack of diamonds.

Jackson slid her cards in. The younger player did the same. He leaned toward Jackson. "I had a hand like a foot."

Jackson scoffed. "Mine was no better. The flop didn't give me anything."

"There's almost twenty thousand different flop combinations."

"Really?"

As the remaining players made their bets, the young man said, "Nineteen thousand, six hundred to be exact."

"That number makes wining sound impossible."

"Math is a card player's friend. It's all about improving your odds."

"I keep track of picture cards and aces, you know, plus my instincts about somebody bluffing. I'm pretty good at that, everybody has a tell."

"Most do, but the pros, we mix it up on purpose."

"You're a professional?"

"Yes. Been at it for over eight years. Started as a senior in college."

"Wow. By the way, I'm Simone."

"Nice to meet you." He stuck his fist out. "I'm Carl."

Jackson hesitated before bumping his fist. She lowered her voice. "You make a living doing this?"

He nodded. "A good one." He tugged at the cuff of his sleeve. "Only downside is casinos blast the air-conditioning." He smiled as the winner of the hand raked his chips in.

"I never saw you here before."

"Just got back to the West Coast. I went to Florida State University and stayed after graduating, but I grew up in Bonita and wanted to come back; my parents still live there."

The dealer slid cards out of the shoe, passing two cards to each player. Jackson collected her hole cards and looked at them. She touched her pile of chips.

A player tossed a green chip in, and the rest of the table matched the twenty-five-dollar bet.

The dealer revealed the flop: six of clubs, eight of diamonds, and nine of clubs. The bet came around to Carl, who picked up three chips. "Seventy-five."

Jackson took another look at her cards and matched the bet along with the other players.

The dealer revealed the turn card, a seven of diamonds.

The bet was to the first player, who knocked on the felt table. The player to his left tossed fifty dollars' worth of chips into the pot. The first player dropped out along with Jackson and another contestant. Carl raised the bet to a hundred. The remaining player looked at Carl and sent two more green chips into the pot.

The dealer turned over the river card, a king of diamonds. The other player groaned. He and Carl flipped their hole cards over. Carl's flush beat the straight and he raked in the chips.

Jackson watched Carl stack his chips. He had six columns. Carl slid them toward the dealer. "Color."

The dealer reduced the stacks to smaller ones, each worth a hundred, and exchanged them for twelve black chips worth a hundred dollars each. Carl dug into his pocket and tossed a green chip to the dealer.

"Thanks."

Carl stood and pocketed the black chips. He said to Jackson, "Good luck."

"Thanks. I hope to see you again."

"I'm going to be back here day after tomorrow."

"Playing Texas Hold'em?"

He smiled. "Is there any other game?" and walked away.

Jackson picked up the hole cards the dealer had just dealt. "Wow, can that guy play."

The bet was twenty-five dollars. She looked at her cards again: a five of clubs and a nine of spades. She looked at the flop cards, remembered that Carl often dropped out early, and slid her cards in.

Jackson had to conserve her money. She needed to figure out a smarter way to play if she was going to get out of debt.

There were YouTube videos touting systems, and she'd bought a stack of books on poker over the years.

She watched the flop be revealed: two queens and an ace. Bowing out early was the right move. If she picked the right strategy and stuck to it, she'd have a better chance at walking away a winner.

As the river card was turned over, a woman sat in the chair Carl had vacated. A quick round of betting ensued. The man to Jackson's left won with two pair: aces and queens.

Another round of hole cards were dealt. Jackson peeked at her cards as the dealer laid out the community cards.

Jackson's heart raced. She was holding a pair of eights. When the bet came to her, she didn't raise, but the woman next to her upped it to fifty dollars. As the bet circled back to Jackson, she raised it to seventy-five.

Everyone dropped out but the new player, who raised it to one hundred. Jackson met the new bid, leaving her with only three chips.

The dealer turned over the flop cards: a jack of spades, a two of hearts, and an eight of clubs. The lady next to her bet a hundred. Jackson said, "Credit." The dealer glanced over his shoulder. The pit boss nodded, holding up five fingers.

The dealer counted out five hundred dollars' worth of chips and set them in front of Jackson, with a marker for her to sign. She scribbled her name and put all of her chips into the pot. "All in."

The woman didn't hesitate, counting out four hundred and seventy-five dollars' worth of chips. Jackson held her breath as the dealer revealed the turn card, a seven of diamonds. He looked at both players before revealing the river card, a deuce of hearts.

Jackson flipped over her hole cards. "Three eights."

The woman smiled and laid down a pair of Jacks. "Three jacks."

Jackson exhaled. "That's it for the night." She stood and looked at the dealer. "I owe you; I'll get you the next time."

She headed for the parking lot, vowing to begin reading *Harrington on Hold'em*. She started the best-selling poker book in history three years ago, but the math in it convinced her she was a visual learner. She went down many rabbit holes, watching scores of strategy videos on YouTube.

Jackson walked into the parking lot. Fishing for her keys, she saw the marker. The five hundred she borrowed put her debt to the casino at forty-five hundred dollars.

It'd only been three months since she cleaned the slate with them. The second mortgage she took out paid off the eighty thousand she owed to two casinos and the fifty K she'd borrowed from her 401K.

If she didn't turn things around, she'd be forced to sell her home when she retired. It'd be back to the crime-ridden neighborhoods and crappy apartments she'd lived in as a child. She threw her shoulders back, promising herself she'd do whatever it took to avoid that.

Two men came out of the casino, laughing and high-fiving each other. As they stepped off the curb, Jackson recognized them; they'd been at the other poker table. How much had they won?

It was the second time she'd seen them celebrating this month. What strategies were they using? Jackson pulled out of the parking lot and vowed she'd read that poker book for an hour before bed.

19

SIMONE JACKSON WAITED FOR A BUS TO LOAD UP ITS passengers. Once the stream of seniors ended, she pulled into a spot in the parking lot.

Jackson reached into her pocketbook and took out a sheet of paper. Reading the poker book was hard, but she'd skimmed through it and made notes.

She looked at what she had written about what to do when you raise the bet and another player raises on top of that:

- *When your bet is reraised, think about how many players are in. The higher the number of players, the stronger the threat.*
- *What are the pot odds? If the pot is a thousand dollars and the cost to stay in is just a hundred, that's ten-to-one, a very favorable situation if you have a solid hand.*
- *How many players are left to decide whether to meet the reraise or not? More players equal more risk.*
- *Is it early? Do you have enough chips to withstand the loss and continue to play?*

She smiled and got out of her car. This was a good start. It wasn't everything, but tonight she hoped it'd be enough to win.

The door slid open, and a blast of arctic air greeted her. She scanned the cashier counter. Going to a woman she didn't know, Jackson exchanged eight hundred dollars, almost her entire paycheck, for chips.

She stuffed them in her jeans and headed for the poker tables.

A male voice said, "Hey, how are you?"

Jackson turned around. It was Carl. "Oh, hi."

"Are you playing tonight?"

"Yes, you?"

"Not just yet. I haven't had dinner. I'm going to get something to eat, you want to come?"

"I ate already."

"Come and have a drink or a cup of coffee. We can talk poker."

"Sure."

They went into the EE-TO-LEET-KE Grill. Jackson said, "You know what the name of this restaurant means?"

"No. But I'm betting it's Indian."

"It's the Seminole word for camp."

"Interesting." He smiled and pointed to the carpeting. "They must like the color red."

"I know." She frowned. "It's almost blinding."

They sat at a table and were handed menus by a server. "Can I get you started with a cocktail?"

Carl glanced at the menu and said, "New York strip, medium well, with a herbal tea."

Jackson said, "Just a coffee for me."

The server left and Jackson said, "That was quick. You've been here before?"

"No. The menu had three strip steaks. Chances are it's their best dish."

"You're probably right."

"I don't want to interfere, but I wouldn't recommend drinking regular coffee when you're playing. It makes you too jittery, and that leads to mistakes."

"That's a good point."

"What do you do for a living?"

"Is it that obvious that I'm not a professional player like you?"

"Don't take it the wrong way, but it is."

"I'm the director of Child Protection Services in Collier County."

"Nice. That's an important vocation."

"It is. What gave it away that I'm not a pro?"

"Don't get creeped out, but I watched you playing the other day, just like I do with all players. Before I sit down and play, I want a sense of who is at the table."

Jackson nodded. "You're a good player. That last hand, when you had the flush, it was played perfectly. You knew you had him beat."

"No, I actually didn't. What I knew was the odds were in my favor. He had a straight, and I had a fifty-fifty chance of getting a flush."

"Fifty-fifty? How do you figure that? When there's four suits, it should be a one-in-four chance."

"That's where keeping track of what's already come out comes in."

The server brought the beverages over. "I'm sorry, but I meant to ask for a decaf coffee."

"No problem, ma'am. I'll be right back."

Carl said, "How long have you been playing?"

"A long time."

"How often are you walking out a winner?"

Jackson shrugged. "Not often enough."

"You can change that, but you'll have to revamp the way you play."

"I'm all ears."

"Well, you have to start with your tells."

"My tells? What am I doing?"

"When you have a good hand, you touch your stack of chips."

"I do?"

"Yes. It's a dead giveaway and sabotages your chance of building a large pot to win. You don't have to win every hand, but when you do, it has to be as big as possible."

"That makes sense."

"I see you're not wearing nail polish."

"I never do."

"Good; it only draws attention to your hands and what you're doing with them."

She nodded. "Any other tells?"

The server set down Carl's steak and Jackson's decaffeinated coffee.

Carl sliced a piece of steak and checked the color. "As close to medium as I'd expect at a place like this." He popped the piece in his mouth and chewed. "The other obvious thing you do is when you check a bet or raise with a weak hand."

Her eyes widened. "What do I do?"

"You slide your chips in forcefully."

"Geez, it's that noticeable?"

"If you know how to look."

"Do you see other players doing the same things?"

"Only the best players can mask their emotions."

Jackson nodded. "I'm going to work at it. Maybe only touch the chips when moving them."

"Or play with them all the time. Just be consistent, so a pattern doesn't make itself known."

"How did you learn to play so well?"

"It took years and years."

"You're only, like, in your late twenties."

"Twenty-eight. But I put the time in to learn the odds of winning and losing hands and situations."

"How much time?"

Carl put his utensils down and dug into his back pocket. He put a deck of cards on the table.

"You walk around with a deck?"

"At least one." He took the cards out of the package and cut them with one hand.

"You make that look easy."

"It is, after you put the time in." He fanned the deck with one hand, put it back, and with his other hand, slinky-like, pulled the cards away and back together again.

"You should do card tricks."

"I can, but unless you get a TV show or something, the money is in playing."

"Ah, do you think you could you teach me? I can pay you, and I won't be a pain in the ass or anything."

"It would take time, a lot of time. Most people don't have the staying power. They may have good intentions, but they don't hang in there long enough to reap the rewards."

"I do. I'm persistent as hell."

"Then why didn't you do it already?"

"I'm going to do it now."

"Why? What changed?"

Jackson leaned in. "Because I'm tired of losing. I had to take a second mortgage out to pay this place, and I'm in a fucking hole. A deep one."

Carl chewed on a piece of steak and stared at her. He swallowed and put his fork down. "Now, that's what I call a motivating factor."

"You'll teach me?"

"It's going to take a while, maybe a year to eighteen months, maybe longer to get some of this ingrained in your playing."

"That's okay. I'm down with that."

"It's going to cost you twenty percent of your winnings. It'll be on a net basis, factoring in the days you lose. You pay me every Friday, no excuses or delays."

"That's fair."

"And don't ask me to lend you money. It's something I never do."

"I promise I won't."

Carl smiled. "All right, then, let's get to work."

20

Carl paid the bill and got up. Jackson stared at the fifty he left for the server, then followed him into the casino. Machines beeping and ringing, Carl said, "Playing the slots is like buying a lottery ticket. I know people make a day of it, but they have lousy RTP rates."

"RTP? What is that?"

"It stands for Return to Player. Most slots run eighty to ninety percent. For every hundred you feed the machine, it returns only eighty to ninety dollars."

"What game has the best return?"

"Blackjack, baccarat, and craps are all around ninety-nine percent, depending on the strategy."

"What about Texas Hold'em? What's its RTP?"

"Poker is different, you're playing against other players, not the house. The house takes a rake from each pot, but that isn't a big deal. You play smart, you can win."

Carl stopped half of a car length away from a poker table. "Now, we're going to watch this table. I want you to study what every player is doing and relate it to the hand they have and what they bet."

"Okay. I'll keep my eyes on their body language."

"Exactly. I'm going to watch the play for fifteen to twenty minutes before deciding whether to sit or not. I don't want you playing, just keep your eyes open. And your ears as well; some players use their mouth to intimidate and distract."

"I will."

"Observing teaches you how players play, and there's always similarities in the things we humans do. It also teaches you patience, which is priceless. Don't be so anxious to sit and play. It's critical you understand who is in the game you're getting into and how the cards are being played."

"How do you remember all the cards? And what about the ones being held? You don't see them."

"Let's keep it simple at this point. We can get closer to knowing the exact odds when we track what cards have been played. For now, we're going to work with outs. You know what outs in poker are?"

"I probably should, but . . ."

"That's okay. Outs are cards that can improve your hand. Let's say you have two clubs in your hand and the flop has two clubs. You need one more for a flush. Since we know there are thirteen clubs in a deck, that leaves nine other club cards, called outs."

"Sure, I know that."

"Good. That's the first step in figuring the probability of winning, called equity, in poker." Carl pointed to a spot on the wall away from the activity. "Let's talk over there."

He leaned against the wall. "Now, there is a lot of math behind calculating the odds. Try and follow me here, I'll keep it simple. In the example we talked about before, you have two clubs and there are two in the community cards. There are fifty-two cards in a deck, and we can only see five of them: your two hole cards and the three flop cards. That leaves us with forty-seven unknown cards."

Jackson nodded.

"Since we have nine chances, or outs, to make our flush, the calculation is nine into forty-seven. Let's round it out ten to fifty, which is twenty percent."

"Right. Ten is one-fifth of fifty. So, twenty percent. I get it."

"Exactly, and not great odds."

"Right."

"But we still have two cards to come: the turn and the river. Let's say the turn is not a club, so we have nine chances out of the forty-six cards left, which is about nineteen and a half percent. That's a little higher than on the turn. The key is to add the two up, so roughly it equates to over a forty percent chance of winning before the turn card is revealed."

"Hmm."

"I can see your eyes glazing over."

Jackson snorted and Carl said, "I know it's difficult, and it's especially tough to figure out when under the pressure of playing. So, let's work with the rule of two and four to simplify things."

"Simplifying sounds good to me."

"Sticking with the same example, you're holding two clubs, and there are two on the flop, leaving nine in the deck. We multiply the nine by four, giving you thirty-six percent on the flop, and by two—nine times two, on the turn—giving you eighteen percent. You can see that equals fifty-four percent, higher but in the ballpark to what we calculated before with all the math."

"I like the shortcut."

"It's far from perfect and just a starting point."

"I know, but the two and four thing is a good trick to help you win."

"It's wrong to think of it as a trick. This is about using mathematics to understand the odds, improving your chances of winning."

"I get it, but I'm excited to be able to know the odds."

"It's a baby step. You can make a nice living on the difference between forty and fifty-four percent."

"I'm sure you can."

"Also don't forget, the example I gave had just two players. Let's say there's you and five other players. The odds are very different because you have to account for the cards the other players have. As well as how they play, including bluffing."

"How do—"

"Not now. Sit with the rule of two and four and keep it in mind."

"I will."

"Let's go."

They stood behind a table, watching the dealer slide cards to the players. After six hands, Carl whispered, "You notice anything?"

Jackson frowned. "Not really. I mean, the lady to the right, she keeps touching her glasses, but I can't see a pattern."

"Keep watching, it might be a tell."

"You see anything?"

Carl cocked his head. "Let's check out the craps table."

Jackson followed him. "I thought you don't play craps."

"I don't." He lowered his voice. "Did you see anything with the two guys sitting at the ends?"

"No. What? Did I miss something?"

"They're playing together."

"They are?"

"Yep. They were signaling what hole cards they had."

"Are you kidding me?"

"When playing for money, you don't kid around."

"I had no idea. I wasn't even looking for anything like that."

"When you sit down at a table, you're in a new world; everything and everyone is in play."

"You saw them do something? What? Tell me so I know what to look for."

"The first guy steepled his hands and was tapping his fingertips together. Then, he'd clasp his hands and go back to steepling and tapping, counting out the value of his hole cards."

"Holy shit. That's crazy, but it's a good idea, right?"

"Cheaters always get caught. Besides, having a partner elevates the risk of getting caught."

"Let's go watch. I want to see if I can detect what they're doing now that you pointed it out."

21

———

THE FURTHER EAST WE DROVE, THE MORE RELAXED I BECAME. A quick trip to the East Coast to collect information on Weiss also gave me a chance to spend some time with Laura and keep a low profile.

Laura pointed east. "It looks like it's raining over there."

"And it's sunny here. The Everglades are so massive they have their own weather."

"Did you ever see an alligator on this road?"

"No, but I guess they wouldn't call it Alligator Alley if there were no gators. These days, the fencing keeps them off the road."

"I thought that was to protect the panthers from getting hit by cars."

"Probably good for both. You know they're having a big problem with pythons out here."

"Snakes?"

"Yeah, they're huge."

"Eww."

"Pythons aren't native to the area, but some people had them as pets."

"Pets? That's disgusting."

"They get so big and need so much to eat that they released them into the Everglades, and the population exploded. Now the balance is out of whack, and most of the native wildlife, like rabbits and foxes, have been wiped out."

"Oh, no. Can't they do something about it?"

"The state actually pays people by the hour and by the foot in length to catch them."

"People do that? Go out and catch them? It's so dangerous, I mean, it's a giant swamp."

"I read they've caught about twenty thousand of them already."

"Oh my God. There's that many?"

"Yep. They euthanize the ones they catch." I saw the sign for the rest area. "You need to stop to use the bathroom?"

"No. I'm good. How much longer until we get to Miami?"

"An hour."

Heading south on Interstate 95, Miami's skyline came into view. "There's a ton of building going on."

"I haven't been here in a couple of years. It looks different. A lot of cool buildings."

"And a lot of traffic."

I turned onto Brickell Avenue. Laura said, "This is nice, with all the trees."

"I'll drop you at a hotel by the water. You can use the bathroom and walk the promenade."

"How long are you going to be?"

"An hour, max. I'm going to be right over there, at the Mandarin Oriental." I pointed to a small bridge leading to an island called Brickell Key.

"That's a cool place to live. I bet it's nice and quiet, and you're steps away from everything."

"I guess so. See you later."

The hostess led me to a table in the shade. Conner Pell stood, buttoning his tan sports jacket. All that was missing was the bow tie. "Mr. Beck." He extended a liver-spotted hand.

"Nice to meet you, Mr. Pell."

"Likewise. Please call me Conner. Sit, sit."

"This is a beautiful spot."

"It is. Nice views, and there's always a soft breeze blowing."

"I appreciate you seeing me."

"A friend of Ray's is always welcome. His father and I worked on the floors of the exchange a long time ago. We came up together."

"The New York Stock Exchange?"

"Yes. Back in those days the floor was hectic, to put it politely. No computers, everything was done by hand, and relationships mattered."

"I've seen pictures of the floor, people yelling and waving papers."

"That's how buyers and sellers were matched. It wasn't the most efficient marketplace, but high-speed trading isn't what it's cracked up to be either. We could use more of the human element. Take a look at the menu. I know it by heart."

I glanced at it. "Just a salad for me."

A smiling server came over. "Are we ready, gentlemen?"

"Yes. My usual, Leslie."

"Certainly. And for you, sir?"

"The Farmer's Salad."

"Excellent."

Music from a yacht grew louder as the boat drew nearer. Pell said, "There's a different element in town. I'm afraid the Miami I retired to is lost forever."

"The only constant is change. There's a saying I like, it might be from Marcus Aurelius: Everything's destiny is to change, to be transformed, to perish. So that new things can be born."

"No truer words have been spoken." He smiled. "The issue is, I'm getting closer to the perish part of things."

"You look fantastic."

"I feel good and stay in motion and engaged. It's the only antiaging defense that seems to work."

The server set down a poached egg and avocado toast for Pell, and my salad.

He was trim. I pegged him to be eighty-five. "Maybe it's the avocado."

He chuckled and tucked his napkin into his neckline. "Ray provided background, and I hope I may be of some use to you. What specifically are you interested in?"

"Again, I appreciate this opportunity, and I wouldn't want to put you in an uncomfortable position with any confidential information you may know."

He stuck a forkful of toast in his mouth and nodded.

"During the time you served on the Securities and Exchange Commission, allegations were made about Melvin Weiss. Do you remember that?"

"Vividly. Mr. Weiss was just coming up. He'd had a couple of minor successes, but it was before the short that made him. Right after I was invited to join the SEC, the commission received a call alleging an impropriety resulting in heavy short activity in Star Enterprises, a medical device entity specializing in replacement joints."

"What were the allegations?"

"Star's stock price had risen on the back of its titanium hip joints. It was an advancement that would extend the life of the replacement."

"They don't use titanium anymore, do they?"

"Thankfully, I've not had any replacements, but I believe

it's a combination of ceramic and a special plastic, called polyethylene." He pushed his half-eaten lunch a few inches toward the center of the table.

Maybe not eating much was part of the secret to staying sharp. "Sorry for interrupting."

"Not at all. Stay curious, you'll never be bored." He removed the napkin from his collar, "Rumors that the titanium was causing high infection rates began to circulate. The stock declined rapidly, and the shorts piled on. Star defended itself, but the newness of the material came with a certain skepticism. A short seller who had been around for decades contacted our office claiming Mr. Weiss had contacted him, asking him to join him in the assault on Star. When he requested proof, Mr. Weiss said it was too early for the infection data to show up."

"Then how did he know?"

"It may have begun as a hunch, but ultimately it was fabricated. Star turned over reams of data showing the use of titanium had no effect. In fact, the data showed infection rates declined slightly."

"Weiss lied?"

"I'm reluctant to characterize it as such. He may have believed it would happen, as microscopic grooves provide a place for bacteria to possibly grow, but the facts are, there was no data to support the attack on Star."

"What did the SEC do?"

He shook his head. "Nothing. We were without a chairman and had another vacancy on the board awaiting Senate confirmation. The board was overwhelmed at the time. I wanted to pursue this, but as the new member, my voice was, shall we say, muted by the acting chairman."

"What do you think should have been done?"

"In my opinion, we had enough evidence to bar Mr. Weiss from the securities industry for life."

22

———

MY LAWYER BUDDY LARSON WAS SITTING AT AN OUTDOOR table at Pinchers in Tin City. Keeping my eyes on the water, I said, "See any dolphins?"

"Not yet, but last week a pair of manatees was just off the pier. They hung out the whole time I ate lunch."

I pulled out a brown sling chair. "I haven't been down here since before Hurricane Ian."

"They got slammed."

"I saw the pictures of Kelly's Fish House. The water was, like, seven feet high."

"The way the community bounced back is a lesson in the resiliency of people in Southwest Florida."

"Yeah, it was amazing. I just don't know how many times I could take getting flooded before moving on."

The server came over. Larson ordered a house salad with mahi-mahi, and I asked for a crab cake.

Larson said, "What did you think of Ruta?"

"If half of what she said is true, with people like Kravitz in Washington, the country is in more trouble than I thought."

"It's no longer public service; they've turned it into a career.

And a lucrative one at that. Do you know they can trade stocks? It's not supposed to be using insider information, but if you believe that, as they say, I've got a bridge to sell you."

"It's depressing. What do you know about Kravitz?"

"More than I wish I knew."

"Really?"

"I wanted you to talk to Ruta, allow you to form your own opinion before telling you what I know."

Information and my time were what drove me, but I let it pass because I respected Larson. "What's the deal with him?"

Larson's gaze drifted to the server carrying our lunch. After the food was delivered, Larson picked up his dressing and drizzled it on the salad. "Kravitz comes from a family with a history of corrupt practices. His father was the president of the Steelworkers Union in New York. He embezzled six hundred thousand dollars, that they knew of, and got away with it. It took three years to force him out, and now he spends half the year in Destin and the other half at his bayfront home on Long Beach Island. And the snake has a condo in Aruba."

The crab cake was good. "He wasn't arrested?"

Larson speared a piece of mahi-mahi. "They made a deal that smells worse than the Staten Island dump. The union defended him—the man stealing from them? What does that say about how deep the corruption is in some of these unions?"

I said, "Like father like son. I don't understand why the congressional inquiry didn't go anywhere."

"It's akin to asking your mother to call you out in public. They protect their own. Every institution on earth circles the wagons when one of their own is in trouble."

"I get it, but not even a censure? A slap on the wrist? How did they get away with not doing anything?"

"By using the time-tested strategy of characterizing a whistleblower as a leaker of sensitive information. It's especially effective when they wrap it in"—Larson made air quotes —"the interests of national security."

"They made Ruta the villain?"

"Exactly, turning the protections supposedly offered to whistleblowers into garbage."

"How'd they do that?"

"Kravitz has a seat on the Foreign Relations Committee. He claimed Ruta released sensitive information on Russian surveillance, when my sources tell me it was Kravitz or his chief of staff."

"But how could they ignore the fact that Kravitz was illegally using campaign funds?"

"First of all, they all do it, not to the degree that Kravitz did, but politicians are always getting caught with their hands in the cookie jar. But in this case, as soon as they invoked national security, the press was locked out. Kravitz started smearing Ruta, and the story went to the leak before dying out."

I swallowed the last of my lunch and tossed my napkin on the plate. "Does he come from money?"

"Depends on how much his father stole."

"His house in Aqualane Shores is worth around eight million. The taxes are twenty grand a month."

"And he has an apartment in the heart of DC. It has to be worth a couple of million, minimum."

"All on a hundred-and-seventy-four-thousand-dollar salary. Does his wife work?"

Larson smiled. "If you count shopping as such."

"I'm going to do a deep dive on Kravitz and could use your help."

Laura and I were on the couch watching a Netflix series. The plot was decent, but caption reading and terrible acting by the Turkish cast made it hard to watch.

I said, "They're overacting like crazy."

"It's not that bad." She grabbed her phone off the cocktail table.

"I thought we agreed, no looking at phones."

"I just want to see when this was made. You know, is that what Istanbul looks like today?"

"Who knows when it was filmed? Streaming services are dredging up anything they can."

She tapped away. "It was made five years ago. I thought it was older. Istanbul has an ancient feel, right?"

"I guess so."

"Why'd she leave the baby with that guy?"

"Makes no sense."

My phone pinged with an incoming email. I stood. "I gotta go to the bathroom." Toby got up, trotting behind me.

After having to remind him, my buddy at Morgan Stanley had finally sent the research report on South Florida Aeronautics, the firm Weiss shorted. I tiptoed into the den and signed in to my laptop using the VPN.

The report was ten pages long. I'd read it without Laura knowing. Morningstar and Morgan Stanley had hold ratings on the stock. They didn't recommend buying but believed the upside was stronger than the downside possibilities.

My glance went to the risk section: *Corporate governance is a wild card. While CEO Whitmore has done an admirable job, questions remain about the skill set required to compete in the unforgiving space industry. The concern is exemplified by their failed foray into supersonic jet travel.*

Whitmore championed investment, allaying concerns expressed by the investor community at an annual meeting five years ago, with a flashy presentation. The projections proved overly optimistic and never accounted for an onerous government regulatory environment.

Exiting the sector led to write-offs that in hindsight should have been taken in one distasteful action.

Whitmore is a solid manager with strong motivational skills. However, the board may want to consider a seasoned hand for its journey into the space sector—

There was a knock on the door. I looked up. It was Laura. "You said you were going to the bathroom."

"Yeah, I went and got a message about work and—"

"Five minutes ago you were preaching to me about not using my phone, and here you are."

"But . . ."

"You're no better than the ten-year-olds I teach." She shook her head and left.

I got up. "Hey, wait a minute."

23

———

A soft breeze was coming off the Gulf. I took my flip-flops off, stepped onto the sand, and walked to Cabana Dan's.

"Hey, how is it going?"

"Busy, man."

"Larson in his usual spot?"

"Yeah, man. Just north of the Ritz line."

Dodging groups of chair-carrying sun worshipers, I walked along the shrub line. Approaching the water-sports setup, I turned toward the Gulf and spotted Larson.

My lawyer confidant was spraying sun lotion.

"Nice day, huh?"

"It sure is." He extended the bottle of protector. "Put some on."

"I'm staying in the shade."

"Radiation is bouncing off the sand. Put it on."

I ducked under his setup. "I'm okay, thanks."

"I got here at nine, and the place was already packed."

A frisbee crashed into my chair. I flung it back as Larson reclined on a chaise lounge.

"You were able to cut the red tape?"

Larson smiled. "Like the mayor of a small town."

"Nice. What did you get?"

He flipped over a corner of his orange blanket, revealing a manila envelope. "Here you go."

I opened the flap and took out a couple of documents. "Kravitz's Congressional Financial Disclosure. Nice."

"You're welcome."

"Thanks for the homework."

After the pod in the Nespresso machine finished dripping, I took my coffee and sat in the recliner. Toby lay beside my chair as I took a sip of java. I reached down, petted his head, and started reading.

The Ethics in Government Act required members, officers, and others to file annual financial disclosure statements. The problem was, like most government rules, there was plenty of wiggle room for the 'home team,' starting with flexible deadlines.

Kravitz's disclosure was almost two years old, even though it was a yearly requirement. That was in keeping with what I'd read; over sixty percent of congresspersons were late reporting their income and assets.

There was also the problem that the report wasn't an accurate assessment of Kravitz's wealth, because a lack of truthfulness and omissions in what was reported was rarely punished. It was the Washington way: write laws that didn't apply to those that wrote them.

Kravitz's Naples home was valued in the disclosure at two million dollars. A quick search on Zillow put the price tag at closer to six million. His Washington place was close to two million.

Eight million in real estate on a hundred-and-seventy-four-thousand-dollar salary? The next section of the disclosure was a summary of the values of his investment accounts. The combined value of securities and cash was pegged at five hundred thousand.

The final section, labeled Other Assets, listed a trust that Kravitz was the sole beneficiary of. The trust, referenced as the Ellie Family Trust, stated its value to be six hundred thousand dollars in real property.

In all, Kravitz's net worth was just over nine million. A large sum of money for the son of a working-class family. He didn't marry money; his wife also came from meager beginnings.

Pulling up the Collier County Tax Assessor website, I checked under Kravitz's name. The only property that came up was his house. I typed in the Ellie Family Trust, and a list of six properties appeared.

Checking each of the properties, all were acquired by the trust within the past eight years. The combined value of the properties held in the trust's name was eight million.

Unless Kravitz, an only child, was the Warren Buffett of Congress, his money was dirty. What he did to Ruta was despicable, but whatever he was doing to accumulate that wealth was an affront to every American.

24

I FILLED TOBY'S BOWL WITH WATER AND GAVE HIM A TREAT. "I'll see you later, buddy."

He followed me down the hallway and turned around when I alarmed the home. Pulling out of my drive, I saw a man duck into a blue sedan. He was parked on the street four houses down. I took my time backing out.

I made a left onto Crayton Road and made another left. The car stayed behind me. I pulled over and the sedan passed me. The driver was a male who looked away as he went by.

Waiting a minute, I continued on my way to Bonita Beach. I turned onto Hickory Boulevard, riding along the Gulf of Mexico for a mile before slowing down.

Weiss's home was still impressive. Parking on the paver driveway, I studied the mansion.

The attention to detail was amazing—and expensive. It was a waste of money, but at least the craftsmen who built it were paid well for the two years it must have taken to finish it. Eyeing interwoven copper belts interspersed in a section of dark wood over the garages, I went to the door.

Wondering what the maintenance costs were, I hit the bell.

The same uniformed woman answered the door. "Mr. and Mrs. Weiss are in the library."

I stared at the Gulf of Mexico; it was mesmerizing.

"Sir, it's this way."

I followed her to an elevator and said, "We could take the stairs."

She glared as if I'd asked her to walk on hot coals. The elevator slid open, revealing a balcony with to-die-for views. She swung open double doors to a darkened, rectangular room. It took a couple of seconds for my eyes to appreciate the Lucite bookshelves, lit from behind, that lined the room.

The king and queen of the castle were sitting in opposite corners of the room.

"Madam, sir, Mr. Beck."

Short-seller Weiss waved me over. "Thank you, Rosa."

"Do you need anything, sir?"

"No. That's all."

As Rosa backed out, closing the doors behind her, Weiss said, "Cynthia, this is the young man I told you about."

Slender Mrs. Weiss put on a practiced smile and came over. "It's so nice to meet you."

According to her DMV record, she was ten years younger than her husband, but she could pass for one of his kids. Maintaining her was probably as expensive as keeping the house up.

"Good to meet you, Mrs. Weiss."

"Please, call me Cynthia."

"Let's sit over here. Are you hungry, Beck?"

Weiss hovered over a table filled with trays of sandwiches, fruit, and veggies. After a light knock, another woman in a uniform backed into the room with a tray of pastries. It was something out of *Downton Abbey*.

"I ate earlier."

"Have something."

"I'll try some fruit."

"Good. Cynthia, would you like something?"

"No. And don't eat too much; we have an early reservation at Butcher."

It wasn't surprising that they were members of one of the private dining clubs sprouting up in Naples.

"Right, I'll have one of these." Weiss picked up half a roll stuffed with meat and lettuce.

I speared a piece of melon and ate it as Weiss devoured his sandwich.

"Mr. Weiss mentioned your passion for horseback riding."

Her face lit up. "I've been riding since I was ten years old. I competed in a host of equestrian tournaments."

"She won quite a few of them. Mostly in dressage, but she also won a jumping event."

"Wow. That's impressive."

"I no longer compete, but my love for riding, and horses in general, will never die."

"A friend of mine is really into it as well. He has a special saddle made by Hermes."

Her eyes widened. "The Hermes bespoke line is magnificent. Your friend must have a good contact as I believe they only take a couple of orders per year."

"He's very well connected."

Melvin Weiss rose and pointed to a corner of the room. "Let's sit over there."

We settled into club chairs arranged around a bamboo table. Weiss said, "We're pleased you're going to write about our philanthropic activities. Perhaps it will motivate other fortunate souls to step up."

Cynthia said, "Melvin, the philanthropic community is infinitely more active here than it was in the city."

Flipping open my pad, I said, "That's interesting. Tell me, what motivates your charitable giving?"

She said, "We've been blessed to be in the position we are in. We consider it our duty to leave the world a better place."

I turned to Weiss. "Is there anything you'd like to add?"

"Well, I agree with Cynthia"—he flashed his mouthful of porcelain teeth—"except the part about luck getting us to the top of the proverbial mountain."

Cynthia crossed her legs but said nothing.

"Beyond monetary contributions, you're active on several boards. Would you like to say something about those roles?"

Weiss said, "Money is important; without it, there'd be no boards to sit on."

Cynthia glared at him and said, "Yes, money is powerful, but without proper oversight and vision, it wouldn't be half as effective. I know it's an old adage, but I'm a firm believer in, 'Give someone a fish and they're not hungry for a day, but teach them to fish and they can feed themselves forever.'"

"So true."

"Cynthia is right. There's not enough wealth to go around, and even if there was, when you give something to somebody it's not valued. It has to be earned, created, to be appreciated."

"Melvin is correct, to a degree, but what about those unable to fend for themselves? Children born into dire circumstances, as just one example."

"Is that why you were drawn to Youth Haven?"

"Exactly. While Melvin and I grew up in lower-class households, we had parents who did their best, setting boundaries, made sure we did our homework, and performed chores around the house. That itself is a gift greater than any sum of money. It gave us a set of values to live by."

A decadent one at that. "As someone who lost his mother and father at a young age, I couldn't agree more."

Cynthia winced. "I'm sorry for your premature loss."

"Thank you. Since your involvement with Youth Haven, the organization has expanded its mission and is serving more children in need. The progress is amazing. What do you attribute it to?"

"As we touched upon earlier, funding is important, but despite the substantial sums we and others have donated, I believe a larger impact has been made by helping to direct and guide the day-to-day administrators."

"You're actively managing the place?"

"No. Nothing like day-to-day management. But the people who operate the facility and its programs are well-meaning and have the children's best interests at heart, but their specialties are primarily on the social service side of the equation. We provide the business acumen to increase the efficiencies necessary to help as many children as possible in a world-class way."

"I've been told you had a hand in revamping their fundraising efforts."

"We take a holistic approach, looking at operations, capital expenditures, recruitment, and fundraising. Everything should be examined with an eye toward improvement."

"I'd love to get an insight on raising money. I just started volunteering with the Guadalupe Center, and they could use help with the fundraising events they hold."

"Good for you. They're a good organization doing wonderful work."

"Any tips you can share?"

"Melvin and I are chairing Uncorked, it's a wine-themed event at Mediterra. It's a smaller event, so we should have time to discuss our approach in real time if you attend."

"That would be great. How do I get tickets?"

"You'll be our guest."

"That's so nice of you."

"It's our pleasure."

"Oh, would it be all right if one of the women I'm working with came along?"

"No problem at all."

I finished up with the short seller and his wife and left. On the drive back, I called a contact named Ginger. She agreed to accompany me and I hung up pleased my plan was coming together.

25

AFTER HANDING OFF MY CAR TO THE VALET, GINGER AND I went into Mediterra's clubhouse for Weiss's charity event. Ginger's backless red dress had heads turning as we walked up to the check-in table. We were given auction paddles and a catalog.

I said, "Let's grab a glass of wine before finding Weiss."

We weaved our way past three buffet tables crowded with food and stopped at one of the five stations where premium wines were being served.

As glasses of cabernet sauvignon from Round Pond Estate were poured for us, I surveyed the room. There were a couple of older attendees, but most people were my age. A crowd of women was gathered by the silent auction items.

I picked up my wine and clinked glasses with Ginger. "To health and happiness."

A voice behind me said, "You want it all, don't you?"

I turned around. Melvin Weiss was wearing a royal blue sports jacket and white linen pants.

"Mr. Weiss."

Eyeing Ginger, he said, "Melvin. Call me Melvin."

"Melvin, this is Ginger. Ginger, this is Melvin Weiss, he's our host today."

He took her hand. "Thank you for coming."

"It's so nice of you to do this."

"It's my pleasure."

"I like your jacket; it goes perfectly with your pants."

He beamed like a ten-year-old who'd won the science fair. "Is there anything Melvin can get for you?"

She lowered her voice. "I realize this is a wine event, but is there a way I can get a vodka on the rocks?"

"Of course. Have you ever had Chopin Vodka?"

"Like the composer?"

Weiss smiled. "It's spelled the same, but it's a super-premium potato vodka. You're going to enjoy it."

"I hope I don't like it too much, because it sounds expensive."

"No worries, dear, Melvin can supply you with whatever you desire."

Her voice went up an octave. "You're so nice."

Weiss put his hand on the small of her back. "Come with Melvin, we'll get you that drink."

As the two of them melted into the crowd, a server came up to me. "May I get you a refill, sir?"

"I'm good, thanks. Do you know where Cynthia Weiss is?"

He pointed. "She's outside on the patio talking to that newscaster from WINK."

I recognized the five o'clock anchor as she headed inside. Hair pulled back, Cynthia was wearing an off-white business suit. I caught her eye and she smiled. "You made it."

She gave me a pair of European air kisses.

"Thanks again for inviting me."

"Anytime. I remember when I first started to get involved in raising money. It wasn't easy, and I ended up just writing checks for what was needed. But I realized if the work that organizations like Youth Haven is doing is to continue after we're gone, it would require broadening the base of support."

"I agree with you. It raises awareness of the mission."

She scanned over my shoulder. "Exactly. Have you seen Melvin?"

"Yes, he stopped and said hello, but someone swept him away."

"Who?"

"Oh, I don't know, they didn't introduce themselves."

"A woman?"

"Uh, I'm pretty sure it was a couple."

Her face relaxed.

I said, "Before I forget, I spoke with my friend Jake, the one with the Hermes connection. I told him about you, and guess what? He said an atelier from France was coming to Naples."

"Really?"

"That's what he said. He'll let me know when, and I'll set up an appointment."

"That would be fabulous. Thank you."

"I'm glad I could return the favor you're doing for me here."

She flashed a neon smile and said, "Let's go inside. We implemented a new idea, and I'd like to see how the silent auctions on those items are going."

A table, fit for a Fortune 500 conference room, was laden with baskets, signs, and clipboards for bids. She ran her finger down a list of bids. I asked, "What have you done differently?"

"We're trying three different tactics, though not on the same items." She pointed a manicured finger at some text in red. "We're asking that bids be made in hundred-dollar increments. We're trying to avoid someone winning by bidding a dollar over the previous bid."

"How much do you expect that to raise?"

"We have sixty-three silent auction items and are hoping to generate four thousand more."

"That's nice."

"We also added three bottles of wine to items that are gift cards to a restaurant. The idea was to be sure a winner took something home with them. It'll probably add a hundred or two to their bids, but it is a good-feeling thing."

"I like that. You mentioned three new things."

"We're experimenting with items that provide a monthly value to a donor and to the business making the gift. Instead of a thousand-dollar gift certificate to a restaurant, we divided them into three or four gift cards. It reminds the winner of the event, and it drives multiple visits to the restaurant. We're even trying it with a nail salon and a dentist."

"That sounds like a good idea."

"We'll see. One thing I can tell you is to test, test, test."

I held up my paddle. "Is this for the live auction?"

"Yes. When we started issuing them to everyone attending, participation in the room skyrocketed."

"People feel compelled to bid."

"Yes, and it may sound crass, but they came to a charity event and, well, we're here to raise money. "

I raised my glass. "Here's to a good haul tonight."

Smiling, she clinked her flute against my wine glass. Her smile crumpled. I followed her gaze. Laughing, Mel and Ginger were heading outside.

"I must speak with a board member. We'll catch up later."

"Sure. Good luck, and thanks again for inviting me."

She headed straight for her husband. Mel quickly said goodbye to Ginger, who shook her tail as she went toward a table full of food.

I circled the room, recognizing five of the women who'd

been to the afternoon event Weiss had held at his home just after my first visit. Women's clothing was something I knew very little about, but I was sure their outfits were several thousand dollars each.

An auctioneer with a microphone said, "Ladies and gentlemen, may I have your attention please?" The room quieted. "The exciting part of the evening is just fifteen minutes away. Get yourself a drink or something to eat and take your seats. If you haven't had an opportunity to bid on a silent auction item, don't worry, there'll be time after the live auction to review the bids on the wonderful packages available tonight. Let me see your paddles, please."

Along with the rest of the attendees, I waved my paddle.

"That's great. Make sure you raise them when the auction begins! We're going to get these children the funds they need to live a productive life. See you in fifteen."

I picked up a sheet detailing the items for auction. As I read, Mel sidled up. "Where's Ginger?"

"She had to leave."

The sound of his crest falling was audible. "So soon?"

"She's something, isn't she?"

He smiled. "She mentioned needing guidance on an investment she was considering. I was about to give her my card when Cynthia came over. She's very sensitive when it comes to other women."

Sensitive, or experienced? "You're the right person to ask for advice."

"I'd hate for her to make a mistake but have no way to get in . . ."

"Would you like her number?"

He cut the smile forming on his face and nodded. "That would enable me to help her. Why don't you email it to me?"

26

Carl led Simone Jackson across the casino floor, stopping briefly at three Texas Hold'em tables before circling back to the first one.

He said, "This looks like an interesting table."

Jackson said, "What makes you say that?"

"Well, I like the mix—two women, both somewhat attractive, and three men around the same age."

"What does that have to do with anything?"

"Everybody is different, but as a species, most humans share basic traits: males will try to impress the females, and the men will compete amongst each other for supremacy."

"They'll play aggressively?"

"Exactly. The women will probably try to take advantage of these table suitors and bluff the men."

"Really? Suitors?"

"Let me rephrase that. Males with money are desirable to most females."

Jackson scoffed. "That's so superficial."

"Yes, but throughout human history, women were attracted to men with resources. Back in time, it meant food, shelter, and protection. Today it may not be as powerful an attraction, but it would be a mistake to believe it doesn't exist."

"In case you missed it, we're not in the Stone Age anymore."

Carl smiled. "Of course not. All that I'm trying to convey is it's still a factor."

"You make women seem shallow, like they're just a bunch of fools. What are men, perfect or something?"

"Males can be just as foolish; status and esteem are powerful motivators. And in many cases, the blind pursuit of being king of the hill leads to irrational behavior. Don't get emotional about it, try to identify it, and take advantage of it."

Jackson was tight-lipped.

Carl said, "You're a social worker, you've studied behavior. There are certain traits present in most of us. Casinos have powerful advantages: they have unlimited money, time, and are emotionless. Therefore, to beat the house, you have to use all the information at your disposal."

"It's not the same."

"I didn't say it was. All I'm trying to get you to understand is people do stupid things trying to get what they want. And once you have more than one person involved, especially in a competitive environment, a lot of, shall we say, jockeying is likely."

"It's true behaviors change dependent on who someone is with. I remember the case studies we dug into on this, particularly with drug use and gang recruitment and activity."

"That's an excellent point. Peer pressure can be a major factor. Why don't we observe for a while, and then if the table looks promising, I'll play."

"You still don't want me to play?"

"Not yet. When you sit down, I'd like you to be better prepared."

"Whatever you say, teach." Jackson smiled.

They stepped closer to the table. Jackson tried to follow Carl's gaze to see what he was studying. After observing the women without picking anything up, she shifted to the men.

They played more aggressively, raising bids more often than the women. One of the larger pots was at stake, and after a round of raises, only a lady in red and a man with a Brad Pitt goatee were left.

The flop and turn cards were made up of an eight of hearts, an eight of clubs, a king of clubs, and a seven of diamonds. Jackson figured one of the players was holding two clubs.

The dealer turned over the river card, a two of spades. The last community card didn't seem to do anything for either player. The woman in red pushed three black chips in.

The man slid a small stack of chips in, doubling the bet. "Six hundred."

The lady pursed her lips and tossed three more chips in. "I'll see it."

They turned over their hole cards. The woman had the flush, but the man made a full house with a king and another eight. He swept the pot in, saying, "Sorry about that."

The apology could be taken as courtesy chatter. But was Carl right? Was there a dynamic in the play? She wanted to talk about it with Carl, but he said, "I'm sitting down. Keep your eyes open."

"Good luck."

Carl snickered. "There's an element of luck, but that's not what makes you a winner."

He settled into the empty chair. Carl was the second player to be dealt hole cards. He peeked at them. The first round of betting started with the player to his left. He bid fifty. It was up to Carl. He slid his cards in, waiting for a better hand.

Jackson remembered the advice he'd given her, that top

players fold seventy-five percent of their hands before the flop. It was something she hadn't done and something Carl said amounted to relying on luck to improve a bad hand. He stressed that starting strong not only improved your chances of winning but conserved cash.

She'd been too impatient and second-guessed herself whenever the flop would have given her a good hand. Jackson watched Carl toss his cards in for the fourth consecutive time. He hadn't spent a dime, and she guessed it was time for a winning hand to come to him.

Carl turned down a drink as the dealer passed out hole cards to the players. He shielded his cards with his left hand and, using his right thumb, looked at his cards.

He called the bid and went on to win a pot Jackson estimated at six hundred. Carl dropped out of the next pot after the flop but won the next three hands.

Jackson noticed something the lady in red did. She couldn't wait to tell Carl but figured he might have seen it as well.

Over the next hour, Carl dropped out of most hands before the flop. He won every hand, except one, that he played to the end and dropped out of six others after the flop.

As the cards were dealt, Jackson counted the stacks of chips in front of Carl; there were nine black piles and two green ones. He was having a good night.

Carl called the preflop bet. The dealer flipped over the community cards, a pair of eights and a king. The player to his left, wearing a ball cap, bet a hundred. The next player raised it to two hundred. Every player but one dropped out. Carl put two black chips in.

The dealer revealed the turn card, a nine of diamonds.

The player in the cap bet three hundred. Carl slid his chips in. The man to his right also met the bet.

The dealer paused before setting down the river card. The

man to his right checked. Carl did the same, and Mr. Ball Cap said, "Five hundred."

Carl moved a short stack of chips in. "Raise it to eight hundred."

The other player dropped out, and the man wearing the baseball hat grimaced as he added three hundred to the pot.

Carl showed his hand, and his competition muttered, "Damn."

Carl raked in the pot and said, "Color please."

The dealer exchanged his chips for higher-denominated ones. Carl tossed a black chip to the dealer, scooped up his winnings, and said, "Good night, folks."

He headed to the cashier, and Jackson sidled up to him.

"You really played well."

"Thanks."

Jackson lowered her voice and leaned in. "The lady in red, I saw what she did—"

"She'd put her hands on her lap when she was bluffing."

"I knew you'd pick that up."

"People think if they act nonchalant, it won't look like they're bluffing."

"I remember in college they said people act fidgety when they're being deceptive. But this was different."

"Exactly. Nice job noticing the tell. That's exactly what you need to do."

"Thanks. Boy, in that last hand, you really sucked that guy with the hat in. How did you know you had him beat?"

"The flop had a king, an eight, and a two, all separate suits. I figured either he had three of a kind, maybe three eights, or possibly a pair of aces as his hole cards. And I was sitting on three kings. When he doubled the bet, I figured it was three of a kind."

"But you called his bet. Why not raise him?"

"I wanted him to think I was chasing a straight or a flush and also wanted to build the pot by keeping one of the other players in."

"Only one hung around for the turn."

"And I appreciated his contribution." Carl smiled.

"Are you going to jump in another game tonight?"

"No. I made enough. Besides, I need a good night's sleep; I'm playing a tournament tomorrow in Miami."

"I wish I could be in one of those."

"You'll get there. You do your homework, and you might be ready for one. I'm eyeing one that might be right for you. I'll tell you when."

"Thanks. And believe me, I'm working on getting better."

"Study those preflops and after-flop hand range charts. You get them down and use the rule of two and four, then you can swim with the most advanced players."

27

———

One of my burner phones rang. I recognized the number.
"Hey Ginger. How is it going?"

"Hiya, Beck. I wanted to let you know that I'm meeting Melvin Weiss for lunch."

"Sounds good. Make sure you stay out of trouble."

She laughed. "I know how to take care of myself."

"You sure do. Keep me posted."

"I will."

I pulled my regular cell out and made another call. "Cynthia, it's Beck."

"Hello Beck. Is everything good?"

"Yes. I apologize for the short notice, but my friend Jake just let me know the Hermes designer is in, but unfortunately it's just for the day. I can get you in, for a saddle, if you'd like."

"Today?"

"Yes, François is leaving tomorrow morning for Dallas."

"I see. Where would this be?"

"The Ritz Carlton at the beach."

She hesitated, and I said, "I know a hotel is awkward, but feel free to bring a friend or two, male or female."

"I ride often with a friend of mine who lives in Port Royal, and she always wanted a Hermes saddle. Do you think it's possible she'd have an opportunity to purchase one?"

"Jake is easily persuaded, and, frankly, he owes me a couple of favors. I'll make sure he takes care of whatever you and your friend need."

"Oh, thank you. I'll call her."

"Great."

"Oh, what time would we have to be there?"

"I told them we'd be there at two. Does that work?"

She hesitated, then said, "Yes."

"Good. And if your rider friend can't make it, bring someone else if that makes you more comfortable."

"Thank you. I think I will."

"Great, then I'll meet you in the hotel's lobby, say at one forty-five."

"That is perfect. Thank you, Beck, this is a welcome surprise."

The Ritz's renovated lobby had a swanky, new-Florida feel to it. A woman was playing jazz on a piano, entertaining diners lingering over lunch and others getting ahead of happy hour.

Rumors ran wild about what they'd spent building a new tower and updating the entire complex, but it seemed to be working.

Phone in hand, I kept my eyes on the entrance. Cynthia and a woman I'd seen at the Youth Haven event strolled in. I sent a text and approached the pair.

They were dressed in knee-length skirts, Cynthia in white and her companion in pink, topped with short jackets. I met them just past the concierge station. "Hello ladies."

Cynthia smiled and said, "This is Rebecca."

Her friend's forehead didn't move as she smiled. "Nice to meet you."

I shook her jewelry-laden hand. "Same here. Are you ladies ready to do a little shopping?"

Rebecca said, "We were born ready."

"Fantastic. François is waiting upstairs."

Cynthia said, "He's not in one of the smaller banquet rooms?"

"No. He took a suite in the new tower."

She took a tiny step back. I said, "Trust me, I understand if you, uh, feel uncomfortable." I motioned to the concierge area. "We'll ask someone to accompany us."

She looked at her friend and said, "No, that's completely unnecessary."

"Great. Let's go."

The elevator pinged and stopped at the ninth floor. I followed Cynthia Weiss and her friend into a wide, contemporary hallway.

"This way, ladies."

I made a left, stopping in front of the third door. The women kept their distance. I smiled and knocked on the door.

The door swung open. Cynthia's jaw dropped. Wearing a white terry cloth robe, Melvin Weiss's gaze bounced between the three of us.

From within, Ginger's voice floated to the door. "Mel, is that room service?"

Cynthia said, "How could you? You little bastard!" She and her friend marched away.

Melvin stepped into the hallway. "Cynthia, wait. This isn't what you think it is."

I walked into the sumptuous, wood-floored room. Ginger

was on the balcony overlooking the Gulf of Mexico. "Thank God. Another minute and I would've had to take off."

I glanced at a bucket holding a bottle. "How was the champagne?"

She grabbed her purse and headed to the door. Weiss said, "What the hell is going on?"

We brushed past him.

"Beck, I demand to know! Did you set me up?"

As the elevator doors slid open, Weiss stepped into the hall-way, yelling, "I'll ruin you, you bastard!"

28

———

I CHECKED THE TIME AND TURNED THE TV OFF MUTE. THE third political ad in a row was winding down, and the news came back on.

A meteorologist was standing in front of a map of Southwest Florida.

Almost as annoying as ads was the endless coverage of the weather. It was a continual loop, fretting about a possible shower with highs in the low eighties.

After providing the current and future temperatures in a dozen spots, the weather woman promised an update and handed the broadcast back to the anchor.

"And now we're going to go live with a disturbing story out of Bonita Springs Beach. Covering it for WINK is Amanda Brighthouse, who is on the scene. Amanda?"

The sky behind the blond-haired reporter was a pinkish red.

"Thanks, Scott. I'm standing in front of Melvin Weiss's beachfront mansion. Mr. Weiss and his wife, Cynthia, are fixtures in the Southwest Florida philanthropic community. However, that's likely to change as the wealthy financier has been accused of filming women in this very home's bathrooms."

The screen split in half, with a shot of the reporter alongside four images of women. "As you can see in these creepy pictures, female guests of Mr. Weiss were filmed without their consent or knowledge. We've blurred the faces to protect their privacy, but WINK News has spoken to two of the women who confirmed they recently attended a charity event at the Weiss home."

The images of the women were replaced by one of Weiss in a tuxedo.

"It's unknown how long the secret recordings were being taken or how many women were captured by the hidden camera.

"Earlier today police searched Weiss's home. Our sources tell us they did not find a recording device. We were told police believe Mr. Weiss was tipped off in advance of the raid. The Collier County Sheriff's Office issued a statement that Mr. Weiss was to be interviewed tomorrow.

"We asked Mr. Weiss to comment on the allegations, but his office referred us to his lawyer, James Stockton. Mr. Stockton denied his client was responsible for the recordings. He claimed they were an attempt to discredit Mr. Weiss and reiterated that no device was found during the search.

"When we pressed Mr. Stockton for information on who was looking to damage his client's reputation, Stockton said Mr. Weiss had many enemies. He went on to say that the primary activity of Weiss's firm, known as Chernobyl, was to bet against the stock of companies Weiss felt were overvalued. The term for such investment activities is known as short selling.

"Our business desk confirmed Chernobyl has come under fire for controversial bets against many firms, including a company in our backyard, South Florida Aeronautics, whose founding family are Naples natives.

"WINK News will follow this story and bring you updates as they become available."

I rubbed Toby's head. "And that's the way you do it, boy."

Popping off the couch, I said, "Come on, Toby, let's take a walk."

I hooked the leash onto his collar, and one of my burners rang. "Hi, Mr. Whitmore."

"Hello Beck. Did you see the news report on Melvin Weiss?"

"Yeah, I caught it. Crazy, right?"

"You didn't have anything to do with that, did you?"

"With what?"

"What Weiss was doing, filming those women."

"If you're evil, evil will befall you. And if you're good, good will come to you."

"You're a fan of Psalms?"

"Not really. My mother used to say that all the time."

"So, you weren't involved in—"

"I've got to run. Have a good day."

"Oh, I will. I'm going to take the wife out to dinner tonight, someplace special, to celebrate."

I tossed the phone on the couch, and we headed outside. Toby tugged on the leash, and I quickened my step. The good feeling that washed over me when the news broke had already started to fade.

Trying to hold on to it, I reviewed the sequence of events that took Weiss down. It didn't help. Why didn't it last? Was it because Weiss was an easy target? His arrogant confidence gave me something to work with, but developing the two-pronged plan and executing it was something few could do.

As Toby lifted a leg near a tree, I considered whether the

satisfaction dissipated because the penalty paid by Weiss, though embarrassing, wasn't fatal. Did I need to cross the line I'd sworn not to?

Back in the house, I gave a treat to Toby and grabbed my phone. I clicked the notification from the *Naples Daily News* and was brought to their home page. There was no missing the lead story:

"Disgraced Financier Questioned by Police"

Melvin Weiss, of Bonita Springs Beach, was questioned by the Lee County Sheriff's Office over photos allegedly taken of women using the bathroom in his beachfront mansion.

The offensive images were leaked anonymously to WINK News and prompted an investigation. Weiss claims to have no knowledge, and his lawyer believes he was set up. A search of the bathroom in question, a first-floor powder room, by detectives didn't turn up any recording devices.

Mr. Weiss didn't comment as he left the interview. His attorney issued a statement that, in part, said they would mount a vigorous defense and clear his client's good name.

I read the next line twice: *Melvin Weiss, sixty years of age, and his wife, Cynthia, have lived in the house where the photos were taken for ten years. The Weisses have been active in Southwest Florida's philanthropic community.*

The pair have been married for thirty-eight years, but the couple recently separated, and Cynthia Weiss, who is now living in the couple's Ocala ranch, has retained a divorce lawyer. It is unknown whether the covert filming was responsible for the split.

The tension in my neck relaxed after realizing Cynthia's pain would probably be short-lived. Was the collateral damage that she'd become, taking the good feeling out of paying it back to Weiss?

She'd be better off without him. Her social life would be

tossed upside down, but the divorce settlement would keep her in velvet for the rest of her life.

Though embarrassed, her husband, Melvin, would still be fabulously wealthy. It was likely he'd move, maybe to Miami, and rebuild his private life. An image of him on a yacht in Biscayne Bay flashed through my head.

The tension in my shoulders returned. Was what we did to Weiss enough? Should he be removed entirely? Weiss had hurt plenty of people, but not physically. And if he had to go, would I be able to do it?

And if I did, would the good feeling that came with getting revenge for others stick?

29

LAURA AND I WERE LINGERING ON THE LANAI AFTER DINNER. I said, "It's so clear out. You can see a million stars."

"Do you think there's life somewhere else?"

"You mean on another planet?"

"Yes."

"I don't know, I guess it's possible since there's supposed to be a ton of solar systems out there."

"You think whatever form of life is out there is more advanced than us?"

I shrugged. "Who knows? Maybe we're an experiment they're running."

"What do you mean?"

"We like to go to the zoo or wherever and observe animals; maybe some alien race is watching us as entertainment. You know, an advanced form of a reality show."

She scoffed. "No, seriously. Do you believe in our lifetime we'll be visited by aliens?"

My phone vibrated and I pushed away from the table. "Who said they haven't already been here?"

I pulled my phone out. "It's Larson. I have to take this."

I stepped into the house. "Hey Ray, what's going on?"

"I thought you'd like to know CNBC is going to do a piece in the morning on Weiss's Chernobyl fund."

"Nice. What's the angle?"

"It looks like institutional investors are pulling out in droves. They can't risk additional issues surfacing on Weiss."

"Is it deadly for his company?"

"Institutions represent about sixty percent of the money he manages. He'll hang on, maybe shut it down and position it as a family office or something like that."

"So, he'll survive it and continue doing what he does?"

"Probably. But I don't think he'd risk playing with facts; any position he takes going forward is going to be scrutinized."

I scoffed. "It won't last, people will move on to something else."

"You did a great job with him. Whitmore may give us a bonus."

"I don't know, maybe we should've gone further."

"You crippled his business and woke up his wife. What more could you do?"

"I don't know, but something about Weiss is—"

"It's over. Move on, you have Jackson and Kravitz to deal with."

"Both of those are rolling out nicely as we speak."

Laura opened the slider and came into the house.

Larson said, "Good, I have to say, the plans seem perfect."

"Let's hope so. Look, I got to run. I'll talk to you later."

Laura said, "What did Ray want?"

"Something about a case."

"What case?"

"It's nothing. Let's go back outside."

"I don't understand why you can't tell me about what you do for a living. It's not right. It makes me feel like a total outsider."

"That's not true. It's just that, you know, there are confidentiality issues, and I can't really get into the details."

"Fine. You can't tell me everything. I understand that."

"Thanks."

She put her hands on her beautiful hips. "Give me a summary."

"It's complicated and involves a lot of financial stuff that I don't even understand."

"Try me."

"Okay. There's a guy who makes money when stocks go down. And he doesn't play fair. He spreads lies and gets others to gang up on the company, so the company's stock goes down."

"Doesn't sound like a nice man."

"He isn't, he also cheats on his wife. And has an ego the size of the Goodyear Blimp."

"What a jerk."

"Yeah. Very full of himself."

"What did you do?"

"We embarrassed him publicly, and he's basically out of business."

"How did you do that?"

"That's all I can say about it."

"Does his wife know he was unfaithful to her?"

"We made sure she found out."

She smiled. "Good. I'm glad she's not being made a fool of anymore."

"They split up already, and this guy has more problems heading his way."

"What do you mean?"

I had said enough. "Nothing, but he's going to lose half his wealth to his wife, his business is falling apart, and who knows what else is going to happen."

30

———

It was good to be alone, in my own bed but my sinus was clogged. Turning onto my right side to let it drain, there was a noise. I froze. Straining to hear didn't reveal anything. It was quiet.

Toby was sound asleep. I relaxed. It was nothing.

Nose clearing, I rolled onto my back and drifted back to sleep.

A tickle in the back of my throat made me cough. Something was in the air. Toby jumped to his feet. Bolting upright, I sniffed—smoke!

Leaping out of bed, I opened the nightstand drawer. Palming my Glock, I said, "Come on, boy."

The hallway was hazy. *Beep. Screech!* A smoke detector went off. I opened the slider leading to the back. "Outside, Toby. Go ahead!"

Toby barked but didn't move. Grabbing my phone off the kitchen counter, an acrid smell burned my nostrils. There was a fire.

I dialed 911 as I searched the house. The hallway to the garage was filled with smoke.

"Come on, boy." Yelping, Toby followed me outside as the smoke detectors screeched.

Motion-sensitive lights lit up the lanai. The grass was wet. Turning the corner of the house, I paused. The garage window was flickering orange. An approaching siren kept me from dashing back inside.

What the hell happened? Was it the car? It wasn't electric and couldn't be a battery fire.

"Holy shit, Beck! Your house is on fire!"

Dave, the next-door neighbor, trotted over.

"Yeah, at this point, just the garage."

"Man, you're lucky you woke up."

"I'm sensitive to smoke. I didn't smell it, but something made me hack."

Dave rubbed Toby's head. "I'll bet he would've gotten you up if you hadn't woken up."

"Probably. Do me a favor and take him until this is over with."

"Sure thing."

Horn honking, a fire truck slowed to a stop. Five firefighters jumped off the truck. "Stand back!"

It took a couple of minutes to put the fire out. The captain of the crew escorted me into the house through the front door. Puddles of water pooled on the kitchen floor. The walls of the corridor to the garage were soaked and marred with black remnants from the smoke.

I was grateful the house had been spared, but the water did more damage than the fire. "You guys came just in time."

"There's a reason code mandates that garage entry doors have to be solid. If not, you would have lost this place."

I peered into the garage. "How did it start? Was it the car or something in the garage?"

"It was intentional."

"Arson?"

"Ninety-nine point nine percent certain."

As I said, "Are you sure?" a pair of police cars pulled behind the fire truck.

"The pad for the garage door was hanging off. They twisted wires to make a connection. It's how they got in."

Would the surveillance camera I had identify who had tried to fry me? "Is there going to be an investigation?"

"Absolutely. We'll nail it down and go from there."

"Okay." I turned around and put my hand on the door handle to a small closet where the electronics were. All the equipment was soaked.

"You'll have to replace all of it. We couldn't take a chance."

"I understand. Look, I got to make a couple of calls."

Phone in hand, I circled around the house onto the lanai. "Mario?"

He answered groggily, "What's the matter?"

"Somebody set my house on fire."

"What the fuck? Who was it?"

"I don't know yet. But you had better be careful. It might be related to something we did."

"A case?"

"That's what I'm thinking."

He snorted, "A payback for a payback."

"Could be. I don't know why it popped into my head, but you think it could've been Mallory?"

"From the fish factory?"

"Yeah."

Mario said, "It's been years. Nah, it can't be."

"You always say the best retribution is the one they don't see coming."

"Yeah, but it's way too long ago. That happened like twenty years ago."

"He said he'd get me if it was the last thing he did."

"Yeah, but he's an old man now."

"He'd only be about fifty."

"I don't see it. Don't forget the Royal-and-Caden thing got you mentioned in the papers."

"That frigging jerk in O'Leary's office leaked it. Though they walked it back."

"What about Royal and his gang?"

"There's not much left of those thugs."

"Royal could be pushing this from prison."

My shoulders tightened. "Maybe."

"He's got nothing to lose."

The reminder wasn't helpful. "We have to put feelers out."

A voice called out, "Mr. Beck?"

"I have to run; the fire captain is looking for me. Make sure you're on high alert."

I walked over to the fireman. He said, "The police want to talk to you."

***

Larson answered the door in a Ferrari T-shirt and gym shorts. "Are you okay?"

"Yeah, thanks for letting me spend the night."

I followed him into the kitchen. "Where's Toby?"

"I left him with a neighbor."

"What the hell happened?"

I put my duffel bag down. "There's no doubt it was arson."

"Geez, you could have been killed."

"I think that was the point."

"Someone's trying to murder you?"

"Looks that way. The cops said the motion-detector light bulbs were screwed loose. They got in through the garage door pad and set the fire by the door leading to the house. It's a good thing I keep it locked."

"A professional job?"

"Hard to say, but they used an accelerator with a bunch of towels and newspapers."

"A lot of damage?"

"My car is shot, and there's water damage inside. I need a new garage door and—"

"That's okay. The important thing is you're safe."

The question was for how long? "I know, but we have to flush out whoever is behind it."

"Who are you thinking?"

"At this point, our old friend Royal might be in the lead. If it's not him, it could be somebody we got back at . . . there's a remote chance it could be someone from way back, but I doubt it."

"Who are you referring to?"

"When Mario and I escaped from foster care, we did anything to survive and got jobs in a fish processing plant on the Delaware Bay."

"I remember that. What happened again?"

"There was this jerk, Bob Mallory. He was the line manager and a mean son of a bitch. He was always pushing me, jabbing me with his stick and screaming in my ear. Everybody said he had it in for me, but nobody knew why."

"Tell me what went on."

I shook my head. "One day, he was watching me slice open fish bellies as the line moved. He was up my ass, criticizing me left and right. When I didn't cut one perfectly, he'd poke me with his frigging stick. I told him to stop, and he glares at me. I get back to gutting and he starts screaming. I told to him to shut the fuck up and he smashes me, right here, where that prick of a foster father hit me. I lost it. I just swung around and stabbed him with the knife I was using."

31

Standing on my lawn, I watched the remediation crew clear debris from the garage. It was hard to believe someone had set my house on fire. While I was in it.

My cell rang. It was Larson. "Hey."

"Did they show up?"

"Yeah. Thanks for calling in a favor."

"Anytime. With all of Fort Myers Beach being rebuilt, everybody has more work than they can handle."

"And the prices are nuts."

"Insurance will cover most of it."

"The adjuster came out first thing this morning."

A dark blue Crown Victoria pulled up, blocking my driveway. I said, "Let me go, Ray. Detective Moreno just pulled up."

We shook hands on the sidewalk. "What the hell went on here?"

"I don't know. I was sleeping and didn't hear a thing. I guess the smoke woke me up."

"Your dog didn't get up?"

"I wish I could sleep as soundly as he does."

"Don't we all. But shit, you're lucky you got up."

"I know. The smoke alarm went off as we were leaving the house, so I would've gotten up."

"I heard it was set intentionally."

"There's no doubt. They got in through the garage pad and used an accelerator."

He shook his head. "Any ideas on who is behind this?"

"Not really."

"Somebody you squared?"

"It might be. There's just nothing that comes to mind."

"What about Royal? He could be reaching out from prison."

"Arson isn't his style."

"What are you talking about? His guys were implicated in the condo building on Cape Coral that went up in smoke a couple of months before Ian hit."

"I forgot about that. But they never arrested anyone for it."

"Royal always covered his tracks until you fooled him. It makes sense he'd try to get retribution."

Was Royal stepping into my territory? "A couple of nights ago, I was walking Toby later than usual. On the way back, I saw a man by the side of my house. He took off before I could get moving and got away."

"Hmm. He could've been casing the area."

"That's what I thought."

"You better be careful."

"I always am."

"I'll tell the captain to make sure he runs a car by here two or three times a night."

"Thanks."

"You need anything? A place to stay?"

"No, thanks. I'm not going anywhere. The remediation guys said it'd take eight to ten days to get everything fixed and inspected."

"What about a car?"

"Enterprise is dropping one off. They should be here any minute."

"All right. I'll check with the arson team and let you know if anything pops out of what they collected."

"Thanks."

"All right, then. Be careful."

Moreno started back to his car, and I said, "Hey, I appreciate you checking in, Moe."

"That's what buds are for."

An hour later the repair crew left, and I jumped into the rental vehicle. It was a massive SUV. I'd driven everywhere and in a lot of different rides, but when I climbed into the Tahoe, an uncomfortable feeling hit.

It was the biggest thing I'd ever gotten behind the wheel of. Was the nervousness related to the size or where it was taking me?

Laura was supposed to come over for dinner tonight. If I postponed it, she'd get mad. If I delayed telling her what happened, she'd find out and things would be worse.

I parked in the lot by Rosedale Pizza and headed for Magnolia Square. The apartment complex had been open a couple of years, and the shine was coming off. Laura had moved into a small unit a few months ago.

Looking up, I saw her. She was sitting on the tiny terrace overlooking the pool. I sent her a text: *Guess who's waiting downstairs?*

OMG. You're here? I'm on the phone with a patient. I'll be right down.

Her yellow blouse was as bright as her smile. "What a nice surprise!"

She wrapped her arms around me. "You've been smoking?"

"No."

"You smell like an ashtray."

"Something happened at the house."

"What? Oh, no. You had a fire?"

"Yeah. In the garage."

She eyed me up and down. "Are you okay?"

"I'm fine."

"What about Toby?"

"He's great. My car is toast."

"What happened?"

"Why don't we sit by the pool?"

She searched my face. "Okay, but what's going on?"

I headed for a round table and opened its umbrella. We sat in the shade and Laura said, "What aren't you telling me?"

"Calm down. There was a fire, and everything is okay. Except my car."

She pulled her lips in. "When did this happen?"

"Last night."

"And you're just telling me now?"

"I had to deal with the insurance guy and get a contractor to—"

"You couldn't call me? It only takes a minute."

"I wanted to tell you in person."

"What time last night?"

Tempted to fudge it, but knowing she'd nail me on it one day, I said, "Around one. I was sleeping and woke up—"

She grabbed my hands. "Oh my God. You could've been hurt or, or—"

"It's okay, everything worked out. Like I said, the car is totaled, and the garage needs a lot of work, but except for a little part of the hallway, everything else is fine."

"I don't understand; how did it start? The car battery?"

"No."

"Then what? Something electrical?"

I shook my head. "The fire captain isn't sure, but he thinks it might be arson."

Her eyes widened. "What? Arson?" She pulled her hands away. "What is going on, Beck?"

"Don't worry, I'm fine."

"Somebody tried to burn your house down, with you in it, and you give me your 'don't worry' nonsense?"

"Everything is fine. Really, it is."

"Do you think I'm stupid or something?"

I reached for her hand, but she yanked it away. "No. Of course not."

"Then how can you say that? Somebody tried to kill you. Don't you understand?"

"Don't be dramatic."

"What would you call waking up in the middle of the night to a house on fire? You can't get more dramatic than that."

"It's not that bad."

She stood. "You either tell me what's going on or I'm—"

"Come on. Sit down, and I'll tell you what I know."

Face in a pout, she sat. "I'm warning you, you better not hold back anything."

I leaned in. "I'm not. Like I said, I woke up and smelled smoke. Me and Toby got out and called 9-1-1. The fire department came and put it out. That's all there is."

"Uh, what about the arson part?"

"Yeah, well, they said it was arson."

"So, now it's definitely arson and before it might have been?"

"I didn't want to scare you."

"Somebody saw the person start it?"

"No, they found an accelerator, like gas, splashed all around the garage, and I never keep gas around."

"How did they get inside?"

She'd make a good detective. "Through the keypad on the outside."

Narrowing her eyes she said, "What did you do to make someone come after you?"

"I really don't know."

"Come on, Beck. Stop playing games."

"Honestly, I've been going crazy trying to think who it could be."

She sat back in her chair. "It's got to be your job or whatever you do for work, right?"

I shrugged. "Maybe."

Laura stood. "If you can't be open with me, this relationship isn't going to work."

"Hey, hold on a minute."

"I've got to go. I've got a Zoom call with school."

32

I parked across the street from Lowdermilk Park and scanned up and down. Just people in flip-flops carrying beach chairs. Mario's low-slung building was so 1970s' Florida. I bounded up the concrete stairs and knocked on his door.

Mario, in cutoffs and T-shirt, opened the door. "Hey, bro."

Despite the low ceilings, my gaze went straight to the view. I stepped inside. "Close the door."

"What's going on?"

"Larson called. He has a lead on who tried to burn me alive."

"Who's the motherfucker?"

"Remember Switzer, the guy from Punta Gorda?"

"Holy shit, He set his wife's car on fire. I can't believe we didn't think of him."

"He was paroled a couple of days before my house was set ablaze."

"We should confront the bastard. Where's he living?"

"Take it easy. The timing could be a coincidence."

"Aren't you the one who says there's no such thing as a coincidence, it's evidence?"

"Right now, all we have is his release and that he's done arson before."

"That's enough for me. What do you want to do?"

"Here's a picture of him. Keep your eyes open. Detective Moreno is going to up the patrols around both our places."

"But—"

"Larson is going to check with his contact at Verizon and see if he can grab Switzer's phone records without a warrant."

"You think he'll get them?"

"All we're looking to know is if he was in North Naples that night."

"Okay. Fingers crossed. If it's him, we nail the bastard."

<hr>

Sun reflecting off the hood, my new ride was sitting on a flatbed. The timing was perfect. I called Laura, who was shopping at the lululemon in Waterside Shops. The driver lowered the bed, and I directed him onto the driveway.

He handed me a clipboard. "I need you to sign the paperwork."

I circled the BMW. "No problem." After a quick review of the documents, I signed them. He gave me my copies, and I slipped him a twenty.

"Thanks. If you have your old plates, I can put them on for you."

"It's okay. I got it. Have a good day."

I put the papers on the passenger seat and went in to get the plate.

Tag in hand, I headed back outside. A truck pulled in front of my house, the painter. I put the plate down and waited for the painter to get out.

"Hi, I'm just checking what needs to be done."

"You're not going to finish?"

"Not today. Probably tomorrow. I have another job on Marco to wrap up. Depending on what needs to be done here, I might be able to squeeze it in tomorrow."

"I hope so. I'd like to get this over and done with."

"You and everybody else."

I took him inside, and five minutes later he was back in his truck.

I knelt at the rear of the car. Screwing the first screw into the plate, Laura pulled up. She bounced out of her vehicle.

"Hey." I pecked her cheek.

"Wow. This is a nice car. The white color is nicer than I thought it'd be."

"I know, right? It's got depth to it."

"The plate is hanging off."

I raised the screwdriver. "I was putting it on when you came."

"Better do it now, or you might forget."

"Okay. Check out the interior, it smells brand new." I knelt as Laura climbed into the driver's seat.

It took a minute to secure the plate, and I opened the passenger door. "Pretty nice, huh?"

She barely nodded.

"What's the matter?"

She picked up the insurance card off the seat and held it up. "Mike?"

"Uh, yeah. My middle name is Beck."

She got out of the car. "There's no middle initial on any of the paperwork."

I wanted to tell her to keep her hands off my documents but knew we'd never recover. "Maybe, but my middle name is Beckstoffer. It's my grandfather's name."

"And I have to find out your real name is Michael by accident?"

"I . . . I . . . I've been using Beck so long I didn't even think to—"

"Stop with the excuses, okay? Ever since we met, you've been hiding things from me."

"That's not fair."

"Really?"

"It's not true. I just like a little privacy."

She scoffed. "You don't think you're secretive?"

"No. It's not like—"

"You don't talk about your family, your job, and you don't use your real name? How do expect me, or anyone for that matter, to trust you? How can you have a relationship with someone if—"

"Come on. Of course you can trust me."

"How can I? When I don't know anything about you."

"You're exaggerating."

"Am I? You never tell me what you really do for a living. For all I know, you could be a drug dealer or something. Everything is so mysterious with you."

"That's ridiculous. I told you about that Wall Street guy—"

"Tell me about your family."

"Let's go inside. I'll tell you everything."

33

———

I took Laura's hand and led her into the house. "You want a drink or something?"

"No."

I went to the freezer and took out a bottle of Tito's vodka.

"What are you doing? It's only two o'clock."

"I feel like I need a drink."

She put her hands on her hips. "What you're going to tell me is that bad?"

"No. That's not it. Let's sit in the family room."

I threw back my drink and sat next to her. The warmth from the booze spread down my chest. "What do you want to know?"

"Why someone tried to burn your house down."

"I really don't know. You have to believe me."

She stood. "I knew it, more bullshit."

"Wait." I tugged on her hand. "Sit down. I don't know, but I have a couple of ideas."

"And?"

I patted the couch and she sat.

"We think it could be someone work related, but we're not sure."

"What do you really do for a living?"

"I help people."

"How?"

"You know, sometimes the justice system doesn't work. Somebody gets wronged, and the system drops the ball. I try and make things right for them."

She frowned. "Either you tell it to me straight, or whatever we have is over."

"I'm trying to."

"Give me a concrete example of what you do."

"I told you about the finance guy who lied to make money."

"Humor me. Give me another example."

"Well, we had a client whose wife was killed in a car crash. The driver was under the influence, but he beat the charges on a technicality."

"That's terrible."

"It is. I can't go into the details; you know, we sign nondisclosures and all."

"So, what did you do?"

"We got him arrested."

"How did you do that?"

"I can't get into that, but he got what he had coming to him."

"Give me another example."

"Okay. I wish I could tell you about the cases we're working on now, but I just can't."

"Are you some kind of private investigator?"

"No, but we do investigate, and we work with law enforcement. In fact, sometimes the police ask for our help with tricky situations."

"That sounds like you're doing things they can't."

"Sometimes."

"That's got to be dangerous."

"We're very careful, and we don't take everything that comes our way. We're very picky."

"You keep saying we. Besides Mario, who is we?"

"A couple of lawyers and some people in law enforcement."

"Is what you do legal?"

"I think of myself as a consultant. I pay my taxes and never got in trouble."

"Except when somebody tried to burn you alive."

"Every job has risks."

"Come on. If you're a bartender, nobody is trying to kill you. Why is someone after you?"

"It could be he was on the receiving end of what we do, but we're not sure. We have a lead on someone, and the police are checking him out."

"The police are helping you?"

"Yes. We work together often."

She grew quiet.

"Does that explain everything?"

"Is that why you use your middle name?"

I hesitated.

"Don't make up a story."

"A long time ago, I worked at a fish processing plant on Delaware Bay. It was a terrible job, long hours and shitty pay, but I was underage and needed the money. A foreman there was a miserable bastard. He had it in for me from day one. He'd pick on me and push me around. He knew I couldn't complain because I didn't have work papers, and one day he went too far, and, uh, I snapped."

Her eyes widened. "You, you killed him?"

"No. We got into it, and I beat him up pretty bad. He was bleeding, and I got scared, so I made a run for it, ending up in Florida. That's when I started using my middle name. It really did nothing to hide me, but I used it and it stuck."

"This was in Delaware?"

I nodded.

"I thought you were from New Jersey."

"I was. It's complicated."

"You ran away from home?"

Technically, I did. "Yes."

"How old were you?"

"Fifteen."

She reached for my hand. "Oh my God. That's so young to be on your own."

"It was okay. It's in the past now."

"It's good to talk about it."

It wasn't. "I survived it. A lot of people go through all kinds of things. It's not a big deal."

"What did you do at fifteen? You couldn't drive or anything."

"We left right before the summer started and went down to Wildwood. We got jobs working on the boardwalk."

"Who's we?"

"Me and Mario."

"You ran away together?"

I was digging up fossils I didn't want unearthed. "Yes."

"Didn't your families come looking for you?"

"Not really."

"Oh. Is that why you were so sensitive about your mother?"

"No. She was a great mom."

"I'm sure she was, but why didn't she try to find you?"

I jumped up. "Because she was dead. All right? And before you ask, my father died too."

It took her a second to piece it together. "You were in foster care?"

I nodded.

"Oh my God. What happened to your parents?"

I sat back down. "My mom was killed by a frigging repeat offender. The bastard was out on bail. My father couldn't handle it and drank himself to death."

Her eyes got watery. "That's so sad. You didn't have any other family to stay with?"

I shook my head.

"No wonder you don't want to talk about it." She took my other hand. "You know, you don't have to be ashamed of anything."

I wasn't. "I'm okay with everything. I'm not saying it was easy, but me and Mario landed on our feet."

"After working on the New Jersey boardwalk, what did you do? You didn't go to school?"

"I had to drop out. But I made up for it by reading like crazy. You know, you can only learn two ways, from another person or from a book." I smiled. "Or these days, I guess, YouTube videos."

"Where did you live?"

"It was easy in a beach town. Me and Mario shared a room in a boarding house, where the lifeguards stayed."

"Ew. It must have been gross."

"It wasn't bad. Besides, the room we had in foster care was like a closet."

"When summer ended, what did you do?"

"We got close to one of the lifeguards, a good kid named Ricky. Mario had told him we were on the run, and he looked out for us. We told him we needed jobs. His brother worked at a fish processing plant on the Delaware Bay, and Ricky hooked us up, even though we were underage."

"That's where you had that fight and ran again?"

"Yes. We came down to Florida. We worked the crops, and I'll tell you, they should make every kid who wants to drop out of school do that for a couple of months. It's tough work."

"I feel bad you had to go through so much. What—"

"I'm trying my best to open up, but it's really exhausting. Can we shelve it?"

"Sure, sure."

"I have to attend a fundraiser for Congressman Kravitz this afternoon."

"Look at you, from picking oranges to going to a political function. How'd you get invited to that?"

"Through a contact of Larson's."

"It's work related?"

"How about we get together for dinner?"

"Sure."

I pecked her cheek. "I'll pick you up at seven."

After Laura drove away, I moved the cocktail table off the area rug and rolled up the carpet. I knelt and put my fingerprints on the safe. *Click.* I swung the door open and removed a stack of hundred-dollar bills. I counted out five thousand, stuffed it in an envelope, and covered the safe up.

34

——————

EVERY SPOT IN THE PARKING LOT FOR LAPLAYA GOLF CLUB was taken. I parked along the curb and slipped into the dining room.

Congressman Kravitz's name, in red, white, and blue lettering, dominated the circular room. Similarly colored bunting adorned the sign-in table. I checked in and stuck a name tag on my sports jacket.

I headed for the deck where Kravitz and an assistant were surrounded by donors. The woman standing next to Kravitz was wearing a light-blue business suit and a lanyard around her neck. She was his chief of staff.

I waited as a smiling Kravitz glad-handed the circle of attendees. My bullshit alarm rang as loud as it ever did. His ability to look earnest would fit perfectly in Washington or Hollywood.

I caught his assistant's eye and smiled. "I'd just like to say a quick thanks to the congressman."

Her gaze went to my name tag. "Of course, Mr. Beck."

"Thanks."

"Oh, that's right, you're a friend of Mr. Larson's."

"Yes. He suggested I get to know the congressman."

"That was nice of him." She raised a finger and whispered in Kravitz's ear.

The congressman smiled and extended his hand. "Mr. Beck, it's always a pleasure meeting a friend of Ray's. How is he?"

"He sends his regards.

"And I send mine. Between the traveling to Washington and my legislative duties, it's been difficult to stay in touch, but you tell him I'm going to do my best to put something on the calendar."

"He'd like that. I know you're busy, but I just wanted to thank you for all you do for our community."

Sunglasses were needed to fend off the glare from his smile. "That's kind of you to say, but it's my job and I take it seriously."

"I know you do, and that's why I'm happy to contribute to keeping you in office."

"We appreciate that. We're going to be in a tight race this fall."

It wasn't going to be close, but you couldn't tell that to the donor pool. "Don't worry, sir, we'll make sure you hold the office."

The assistant tapped his shoulder. "Congressman, it's time to get things underway. Cory needs a word with you before you begin."

Kravitz said, "Thanks, everyone. I've got to kick things off."

As Kravitz headed to the corner, I stepped in front of his assistant. "I'd appreciate a quick minute in private."

"Uh, we're about to—"

"It's about a donation."

"Sure."

I followed her to the lobby. My back to the room, I pulled

an envelope out of my breast pocket. "Here's a contribution." I lifted the tab, showing her a bunch of bills. "There's five thousand in here."

She paused.

"I'm old school. Got it from my father; he never trusted banks."

She scanned the area and took the envelope. Stuffing it into her purse, she said, "Thank you. We'll mail you a receipt."

"That won't be necessary. I just want to help him get reelected."

"We're grateful for your generous donation."

"There's more where that came from."

"May I ask what you do for a living?"

"I'm an advocate for several businesses that appreciate the work the congressman is doing."

"Are you a lobbyist?"

"You could say that."

"What firm are you with?"

I handed her a card. "I'm connected to Winter and Partners."

She scrunched her face. "I don't know them. Are they based in Washington?"

"No, we're a small, local company. And don't worry, we focus on Florida issues and never work on behalf of a foreign entity or government."

She smiled and headed back through the open doors. I watched her wait until Kravitz was done talking. She whispered in his ear. Nodding, the congressman's line of sight landed on me. I gave him a thumbs-up and headed to my car.

Leaving the car door open, I put the air on full blast and called Larson. "Hi, Beck."

"Are you still on the beach?"

"No, I got home an hour ago. What's going on?"

"I met Kravitz and handed one of my Winter Partners cards to his assistant."

"Good. Mary knows what to say if they call."

"Not if, They're going to check me out."

"No problem, it's covered."

Mind on Kravitz, I set the takeaway bags on the counter. Laura said, "Inside or out?"

"I'd rather eat outside. Let me wipe the table down. Grab the napkins and utensils."

Laura lifted the Styrofoam clamshells out and handed one to me. "This is the branzino."

She stabbed a piece of fish out of her meal. "Nemo makes the best snapper salad."

"That place is always good."

"It's frantic during season, but the food is always consistent."

"As consistent as a politician lying."

"What?"

"Just saying, you can count on them, like a politician giving you a line of bullshit."

She shook her head. "Can I have the olive oil?"

Passing the bottle to her, my cell rang. "I need to get this."

I stepped to the edge of the lanai. "Hey, Moe. What's going on?"

"It wasn't Switzer."

I was certain it was the guy I'd testified against. "You sure?"

"Yes. His phone records show him being in Lee County."

"He could've left it home."

"Switzer moved around that night but never crossed into Collier."

"Damn. I thought it was him."

"It doesn't look like it. Any other ideas?"

"I'm starting to think it might be someone from way back, before I got down to Florida."

"Who?"

"I'll tell you when I see you. Thanks for checking into Switzer."

I turned around, and Laura was standing behind me. "Who was that?"

"Detective Moreno."

"Who's Switzer?"

She'd make a great interrogator. "Remember I told you about the case I had and the guy I thought might have been the one to start the fire?"

"Yes. The man who burned his ex's car."

"Yeah, but he wasn't in the area that night."

"They tracked his cell phone?"

I had to be careful around her. She could piece things together "Yes."

"So, who do you think it was, then?"

"I don't know."

"You just told the detective it was someone from way back."

"Can we finish eating?"

She put her hands on her hips. "You told that cop it was someone you knew. Who is it?"

"I'm not sure, but it could be that foreman at the fish plant I worked at."

"The guy you beat up?"

"Yeah."

"Why would he come after you now, after all these years?"

"Sit down."

She sat. I said, "This was a long time ago. I was barely sixteen, and we had just gotten jobs working a line, and the foreman, this punk, Mallory, took advantage of me and Mario, but he had it in for me."

"You told me about him. I don't get it, you beat him up years ago. Why would he come after you now?"

"I don't know. He just doesn't like me. He'd always give me the shittiest job and was constantly on my back. He had this walking stick or whatever it was with him, and he poked me, like twenty times a shift."

Her eyes narrowed. "You going to tell me what really happened?"

"Okay, okay. One day he was on me as soon as the line started up. I was gutting fish."

"Ew."

"You get used to it."

"I wouldn't."

"Well, that day, he was right behind me, criticizing me, like nonstop. He poked me a few times, and then he hit me on the side of the head. Right where my scar is, and I just lost it."

"That's terrible. Did you hit him back?"

I looked at my hands. "I stabbed him."

"Oh my God. You, you killed—"

"No. No, I didn't kill anybody. I hurt him bad, really bad. He survived."

"Did you get in trouble?"

"I took off. Me and Mario went to Atlanta for a while and then came to Florida."

"And that's why you started going by your middle name?"

She could be a real help on some of the cases I took on. "Yeah. I mean, in Atlanta I washed dishes under a fake name, but when I came down here, I just used Beck."

"Aren't the cops looking for you?"

"No. Mallory never filed a complaint or anything. I mean, it was self-defense, but I couldn't take the chance. He was the boss, and I was just a kid."

"Why do you think it's him?"

"He said he'd get me if it was last thing he ever did."

35

———

My cell rattled on the nightstand. I grabbed it and jumped out of bed. It was an alert from my surveillance system. Somebody was at the front door of my house.

A male in a hoodie was peering into a front window. Who was it? The black-and-white image was grainy. The man moved to the side of the house and was picked up by another camera. His limp brought to mind someone in Royal's gang.

Laura propped herself up. "Beck? What's the matter?"

I went to the far corner of the hotel room. "Nothing. Go back to bed."

"What is it?"

"Nothing. Just a notification from the camera app. It looks like a malfunction."

"Come back to bed."

"In a minute." I dialed the front gate. "Hey, this is Beck. Can you run a car by my house? It looks like someone might be trying to get in."

"No, no. I'm in Miami."

"Let me know." Before I could disconnect the call, Laura was out of bed.

"Someone's by your house?"

"I don't know. Just trying to make sure, that's all."

"Don't lie to me! You told them someone was trying to get in."

"Take it easy."

"Take it easy? Someone is after you and I'm supposed to take it easy?"

"Calm down. It's—"

"Oh, now I know why we came to Miami, to run from someone who's after you."

"No. That's not true."

Hands on her wonderful hips, she said, "Well, tell me what's going on, or I'm leaving."

"Leaving? Did you forget you're in Miami?"

"What do you think, I can't take care of myself?"

"Of course not." I stepped toward her, but she backed away.

"If you don't tell me what's going on, I'm out of here. And it'll be for good, and I mean it."

I put my hands on her shoulders. "Okay, okay. Just relax and I'll tell you."

She sat on the edge of the bed. As I dragged a chair over, a siren screamed from the street below. Their timing sucked.

"I want it straight this time, no sugarcoating."

"The truth is, I don't know who the hell is after me."

"Great. Somebody tried to burn you alive, and you expect me to believe you don't know who it is."

"If I knew, I'd take action. I'd let my friends in the police know. You think I want to be a sitting duck for whoever it is?"

"It's work related, right?"

"It could be. But I honestly can't figure out who."

"Tell me your top three guesses and why they'd want revenge on you."

If there was a fire alarm, I'd pull it. "If it's anybody, it could be one of two people."

She leaned forward. "Who and why?"

"Well, one guy, he's a crooked doctor. He'll make up anything to get money out of companies."

"What did you do to him?"

"Uh, we, uh, shut him down."

Her eyes widened. "You killed him?"

"No, no. I don't do stuff like that. We just caught him in the act. I went kind of undercover and said I slipped at Walmart, and he said he'd get me an MRI to show damage and all kinds of nonsense. We exposed him, and he lost his license to practice medicine."

"Oh. You think a doctor would try and kill someone?"

"He could've hired a professional."

"An assassin like we saw on that Hulu series? In Naples?"

I didn't want to tell her that all the sunshine we had also cast shadows that concealed a world of crime and danger. "It sounds crazy, but other than him, it could be the guy I told you about in Delaware."

"Why do people feel the need to get revenge when they are the ones who started things? I mean, that bully at the fish processing plant, he kept harassing you."

Harassing wasn't even a word back then. "It's human nature to get even."

"Human nature? It's destructive, that's what it is. Holding a grudge is letting someone live in your head rent free."

That made me a landlord. I sat next to her on the bed. "Anyway, that's what's going on. Okay?"

She grabbed my hand. "No. It's not okay. Someone is after you. It's not safe going home. We should stay here."

"In Miami?"

"Yes, until this is over. I have my laptop and can work from here."

Running wasn't in my DNA. "That's not going to solve anything. If I'm not around, we'll never find out who it is."

"So, you're going to be a piece of bait?"

"That's not how it is."

"Really? Then how is it?"

"I've got the police looking into the doctor and Mallory, the guy from Delaware. Nothing is going to happen."

"You could stay at my place until they catch him."

"Thanks, but it's not at that point."

"So, unless you're in imminent danger, you don't want to stay with me?"

"That's not how it is, and you know it."

"Then why haven't you ever stayed over at my place? Not even one time?"

"It's just easier when you come over to me. I have a house. Hold on." My phone vibrated. It was the security guard from my neighborhood. The call was quick, and I hung up.

"They couldn't find anyone."

"Did they check the video?"

"They did, nothing showed."

"It's an inside job."

She was an Olympian gold medalist in jumping to conclusions. "It's not a neighbor. Somebody could've jumped the fencing."

"Didn't anybody see anything?"

"Come on, let's get back to bed."

"I can't sleep with this going on."

I kissed her shoulder. "Perfect. Since we're up, I know what we can do."

36

———

Traveling south on Route 41, I made a right onto Bayshore Drive and pulled into one of the strip malls that carpeted Southwest Florida.

Sandwiched between a Big Lots and the Grand Buffet was a storefront housing the office of Marty Kravitz, Florida's 19th Congressional District representative. The windows were covered with posters of the congressman, all using the colors of the US flag.

Patriotism was a theme used by most politicians. It was warmly received in Southwest Florida, but the truth was it wasn't about what was good for the country but what benefited the politicians and the business interests that lavished money on them.

One of the four impeccably groomed twentysomething-year-olds behind desks popped out of their seat. "Welcome to Congressmen Kravitz's office. How can we assist you today?"

"I have an appointment with Mr. Kravitz."

"Fantastic. Are you a constituent of the congressman?"

"Yes."

He handed me a clipboard. "We need you to sign in."

"Okay."

"I'll check with the congressman."

Did he enjoy saying that word? Did it make him feel important?

Taking my suit jacket off, I filled out the sheet. Certain I'd be inundated with requests to donate to his campaign, I used a Yahoo email account I checked monthly. I handed off the clipboard and was shown into Kravitz's office.

The office was cramped with a desk, a credenza laden with photos of Kravitz with the president and various senators, and two chairs.

His handshake was firmer than I remembered. "Good to see you again. Sit. Can we get you anything?"

I stole a look at a piece of paper in the center of his desk. It had my name on it. "No, I'm fine."

"Thank you for your donation. Running a campaign is incredibly expensive these days."

"I'm sure it is. Inflation has ramped up the costs on everything."

He glanced at the document. "How can we help you today? Is it regarding the shelter you spoke to my staff about?"

"Yes. I think it's something the community needs and that Washington should get behind."

"Tell me about what you're trying to do."

"Well, we can do it, if we can get the funding. Now, I know you sit on the Ways and Means Committee, and they control the purse strings of the federal government, right?"

He straightened his shoulders. "Not all of it, but most of the discretionary spending must go through our committee."

"It's no secret many women are abused by their partners and are without the financial means to leave them. We want to provide a safe haven for these battered women as our first priority."

"It's a worthy idea, but the county already has The Shelter for Abused Women and Children, which HUD, Housing and Urban Development, helps to fund. I don't know what the appetite would be for duplicating that."

"They're a wonderful organization, but we believe the market is underserved. The Shelter for Abused Women has two sixty-bed facilities, one in Naples and the other out in Immokalee. Last year, the Collier County Sheriff's Office responded to two thousand calls on domestic violence."

He wagged his head. "A sad and enormous number, but I'm not sure those calls result in a need for sheltering."

"Our studies have shown that if the option was available, more women would take advantage of it."

"A small but growing contingent of members is looking to kill duplicate programs. I'm afraid something like this might be a difficult sell."

"I have confidence you'll be able to convince your colleagues to fund this vital project."

"How much money would be necessary to build a facility?"

"Less than it should be, because the property is being donated. We have a firm bid from a builder who built a similar facility in Sarasota. We're using their plans to save money and speed things up."

"Smart. How much will it cost?"

"Twelve million, a drop in the bucket in Washington."

"Have you explored what the county could assist with financially?"

"They're tapped out, but the State of Florida said if the Feds were involved, they'd match up to two million."

"So, you need ten million?"

"Yes. It's cheap, especially today."

"This is going to take time. The federal government moves

at a glacial pace. I'll need to find a reason to motivate my fellow committee members."

I pulled an envelope out of my pocket and set it on his desk. "Here's an incentive to move things along."

Kravitz looked at the door, which was closed. "We can always use campaign contributions. Thank you." Lifting the flap, he peeked at the stack of fifties before sweeping the envelope into a desk drawer.

"You're welcome."

I leaned forward and lowered my voice. "If cash is a problem, I have a couple of options, none of them traceable."

"Interesting." He pointed to where he put the envelope. "Things like this need to be digestible."

"You'll never get agita from me."

Kravitz smiled. "Then we'll get along just fine."

"I'm looking forward to a long, mutually beneficial relationship."

He sighed. "That's the problem with Washington, everybody wants a one-sided deal."

The capital's problem was there were too many people like Kravitz there. "That's unfortunate. So, how quickly can you get this moving?"

"Let me test the waters. Once I determine the appetite of the committee, I can provide a better picture of the funding possibilities. But as mentioned, it's doubtful."

"You have a record of doing what's good for your constituents, and this fits the bill."

"I'm proud of what we've been able to accomplish; however, and I'm not making light of the situation of too many women being abused, there are already existing programs to deal with that population."

I stood. "Thank you for your time, Congressman. When will I hear from you?"

"I'm heading to Washington tonight. Give me a couple of days."

I stepped into the sunshine. My phone vibrated again. It was Susan, Mario's girlfriend. I sent a text: *I'll call you back when I can.*

She replied: *Mario is in the hospital.*

I dialed Susan's number. "Hey, what's going on?"

"Can't talk, the doctor just walked in. We're at the North Naples NCH."

"Did somebody attack him?"

Click.

"Hello? Susan?"

She hung up. I jumped in my Beemer. Had the same people who set my house on fire gotten to Mario?

37

I skidded into a spot and dashed to the hospital's emergency room entrance. Mario was in room four. I paused before looking behind the curtain.

Wearing an oxygen mask, Mario was asleep. As Susan jumped to her feet, I scanned his body. There weren't any physical signs of an attack.

Susan hugged me and started crying. I said, "What happened?"

"They say he overdosed."

"Overdosed? Are you sure?"

"That's what they said. I found him on the floor, and he was having a seizure or something."

"How much was he using?"

"Not that much."

"Stop the bullshit. He's here for a reason. Was it coke?"

"He really doesn't do it a lot. At least that I know of. I mean, he smokes too much weed, but that's about it."

"Open your eyes. I knew he was snorting that crap. I told him to lay off—"

A woman in a white gown stepped in the area. "Hello, I'm Dr. Varita."

I said, "Hi. Are you sure Mario overdosed?"

"I'm afraid so."

"On cocaine?"

"Yes. We ran a screen, and it came back positive."

"How much was he doing that he OD'd?"

"It's difficult to determine. The risk of overdose is wildly unpredictable. Someone can overdose on a tiny amount, while others tolerate higher levels before succumbing."

"What happened to him?"

"Cocaine use poses a significant risk to your neurological system, and in your friend's case, it resulted in a seizure. It could have been worse; we've seen too many users slip into comas."

"From fentanyl?"

"Not just from fentanyl. Cocaine alone can induce a coma. It's a dangerous drug."

"People are crazy taking any of that crap."

"Your friend is lucky he didn't suffer cardiac arrest. Heart attacks are a major risk as cocaine severely impacts the heart's rhythm. He suffered a seizure."

I shook my head. "He'll be all right, won't he?"

"If he stops using, he'll be fine."

"Any lingering effects?"

"We don't believe there will be any long-term consequences from this. But it was a close call."

Susan said, "I hope so. How long does he have to stay here?"

"We'll keep him overnight as a precaution. If he remains stable, he'll be able to go home tomorrow morning."

"Okay. Thank you."

The physician removed her glasses. "We strongly encourage

your friend to seek professional help. Dealing with addiction is complicated. The hospital can recommend several good places in the area."

Susan said, "Okay, Doctor, I'll ask him."

The doctor nodded. "It's very important he get the counseling he needs."

"I hope he agrees."

Hope, there was that word again. Hope was nothing but a prison for the lazy. Hoping never accomplished anything. You had to prepare, plan, and act if you wanted something. Hoping left things to chance.

The doctor left. I turned to Susan. "Mario has to get help."

"He's not that bad. He only does it every now and then."

"He's an addict."

"No, he's not!"

"Did you hear what the doctor said? He's got to go in a program."

"He's not going to want to go."

"Do you know his mother was on crack when he was born? He had to be weaned off like an addict."

She frowned. "He told me."

My phone vibrated. "I have to get this, it's Larson."

I stepped into the hallway. "Hey Ray. What's going on?"

"I heard Mario is in the hospital."

His network was better than I thought. "Yeah, he was screwing around with coke and had a seizure. But he's okay now."

"Jesus. Why the hell is he screwing around with that garbage for? With his history—"

"I know. I'm going to get him into a program so he gets the help he needs."

"I have a contact at Celadon. I'll set it up."

"Oh, man, that would be great."

"No problem. I'll speak to them and let you know."

"Thanks, man."

"Hey, I wanted to let you know that Kravitz was checking into you. He called Winter and Partners, and they verified your cover."

"Perfect."

Mario was sitting on the hospital bed tying his sneakers. My foster brother smiled when he saw me come in.

I embraced him. "Hey, bro. How are you feeling?"

"Perfect. Ready to get the hell out of here."

"Good. They release you?"

Susan said, "Yep, he just signed out."

"Great. Let's get rolling."

Susan said, "I have to take my mother to the doctor. I'll meet you back home."

Mario kissed her cheek. "Okay, see you later."

I led Mario to my car. He got in and said, "I'm starving, the food in that place is terrible."

"Everybody said it's a lot better than it used to be."

"It's still hospital food. Let's go to North Naples Country Club. I'm dying for a smokehouse burger."

"I know a better place in Fort Myers."

"Where?"

"You'll see."

We crossed into Fort Myers and drove along Palm Beach Boulevard. Stopped at a light on Freemont Street, I tapped out a text. I turned, driving toward the water.

"This place on the water?"

I pulled the sun visor down. "Yep. It's got incredible views."

I pulled into a circular driveway servicing the Celadon Recovery Campus.

"What the hell?"

"Take it easy."

"I'm not going in there!"

"We talked about this last night. It'll be good for you."

"I said I wasn't going. I don't need this bullshit."

I grabbed his arm. "Come on, buddy, admit it, you got a problem, and this place is going to help you beat it."

"I'll deal with it on my own."

"Listen to me, bro. Why would you want to struggle? You got to use all the tools available."

"I can do this myself."

"You probably could, but why take the risk? Why string things out?"

"No, man. Come on. You know I—"

"You got to trust me. You trust me, right?"

"Yeah, man. But this is crazy."

"If you don't want to do this for yourself, then do it for me. I can't lose you, bro. Okay?"

He hung his head. "How long I gotta be here?"

"It's up to you. You make progress and you're out in thirty days."

"Thirty days! That's way too long."

"Time flies."

"I got nothing with me."

"Susan is getting your clothes. It's going to be all right. Come on, let's get this over with."

Mario's lip quivered. "Are you and Susan going to come see me?"

"Of course." I couldn't tell him Celadon would determine when he'd be allowed visitors.

He took a deep breath and opened the door. "Okay. I'm ready."

Approaching the entrance, a linebacker of a man came out of the facility. "Welcome to Celadon. My name's Paul, I'm the director."

"Thanks. I'm Beck, and this is Mario."

We shook hands and Paul said, "We've got it from here, Beck. Come on in, Mario, I'll show you around. You're going to enjoy your stay with us."

Mario looked at me. I blinked back a tear. We embraced. I said, "You're going to be fine, bro. I'll see you in a day or so."

Stomach swirling with snakes, I hustled to my car and looked over my shoulder. Mario disappeared into the facility. I couldn't help feeling guilty. It was for his own good, but I felt like shit leaving him there.

I couldn't shake the look on his face. It was the same forlorn expression Bev had when we left her behind in foster care. I pounded the dashboard. How the hell did it get this far? Would he beat this or slide further into a drug abyss?

38

A soft, warm breeze was helping a father and son lift a yellow kite into the sky, and a couple of families were enjoying a late afternoon picnic on Baker Park's expansive lawn. My heart tugged at the simplicity of the interactions.

Would I ever get there? A ringing bell had me sidestepping off the walkway. A man who looked like Larson was bicycling with his daughter.

I watched them pedal away, thinking Larson seemed happy with the little things in life. He enjoyed sitting on a beach and had a fat bank account. Larson wasn't a loner, but he seemed to have found peace, even after his wife died. Was seeing his son, Tommy, from time to time enough?

Larson rarely dated and was content with his life. Wondering how he did it, I saw Kravitz walking from the parking lot. I put my glasses on and approached him.

We shook hands. "Good to see you, Congressman."

"Same here. I haven't been here since the dedication."

Why come if there was no press coverage? "They've done a lot. Let's walk to where it's quiet and we can talk."

We stepped onto the boardwalk. The sun bounced off the

Gordon River as we arched over it. Kravitz said, "This is a beautiful amenity for the community."

"It is, and so would the shelter I proposed be."

"You're very determined, aren't you?"

"That's an understatement. For me it's personal."

"Your mother?"

I took a deep breath and shook my head.

"A sister?"

My foster sister, Bev, and my mother flashed through my mind. "No. I lost two close friends to domestic violence."

"Two of your friends were murdered? How tragic."

He almost seemed sincere. "Technically, it wasn't murder, but Jeanine turned to drugs to escape the world she was living in, and Christine hung herself."

"Jesus, that's terrible."

They were lies but within the realm of possibilities of what might have happened to Bev and Mrs. Bryant. "They felt trapped. If they had a place to seek refuge, they'd still be around."

"I understand why the shelter is important to you. I wish I could help, but my fellow committee members don't see the need to prioritize this at this time."

We stepped off the boardwalk onto an asphalt path. "That's unfortunate. What is the problem?"

"There's a long list of things. Let's just say the timing isn't ideal."

I stopped walking and faced Kravitz. "As I've said, the idea of providing a safe haven is close to my heart, and I'm more than willing to help you convince your colleagues it's an urgent need."

Kravitz scanned the area before saying, "Incentivizing them would be an expensive endeavor."

"We understand."

"How much are you prepared to spend? I need to spread the money around."

I leaned into him. "For a ten-million-dollar grant, you get a hundred thousand. If you can swing twelve million, I'll up it to a hundred and fifty."

Kravitz smiled. "A hundred for ten million? That's one percent. It hardly qualifies as a finder's fee."

"What do you want?"

"Three hundred thousand for ten, four hundred if I get twelve million approved."

I hesitated. "Sounds fair, but getting that kind of cash is a problem for me, and frankly, it'd raise flags."

"I can handle it, but it's crucial we stay under the radar."

"It'd be tough. What I can get my hands on are diamonds."

"That's an interesting idea. I've never used them before."

"I use them all the time. They store tremendous value in a small package."

"I'll have to think about that."

"Trust me, they're used all the time. The feds don't track them like they do cash."

Kravitz nodded slightly. "Okay. I'll give it a go."

"Good. When will you get your colleagues on board?"

"I'll have some upfront expenses. There are people I need to take care of. I'm going to need an advance."

"How about ten grand."

"Make it twenty, and that has to be cash."

I stuck my hand out. Kravitz shook it, saying, "Good doing business with you."

"The pleasure is mine, Congressman."

39

TOBY STARTED BARKING AS I WALKED UP TO LAURA'S apartment. She opened the door and Toby jumped up.

Laura said, "He knew you were here before you rang the bell."

"Hey, boy. Did you have a good time at Laura's?"

"Toby was great. He's so easy."

Kneeling, I scratched his ear.

"Come in. I made lunch."

I nodded and stepped inside.

She opened the fridge, took out two dishes, and set them on the table.

She said, "What's the matter?"

I followed her inside. "Nothing."

"You haven't said two words since you got here. What's going on?"

I shrugged.

"Tell me what's the matter?"

"I had to take Mario to a drug rehab place."

"What? He's an addict?"

"No. He was just doing a little too much, and it's better to nip it in the bud before it gets out of control."

"I don't understand. Why go to a rehab facility if you don't have a problem? Those places are expensive."

"I made him go."

"You made him? Why would he agree to something like that?"

"He OD'd the other night."

"Oh, my God. What happened?"

"He's super sensitive to cocaine and he had a seizure."

"Is he all right?"

"He'll be fine, as long as he stays away from that crap."

"You're a good friend."

"He's more than a brother to me." I whispered, "I can't have anything happen to him."

She took my hand. "Mario's going to be fine. Nothing is going to happen to him."

"I should've done something sooner."

"You knew he was using?"

"I guessed it but figured it wasn't a big deal. I told him to cool it but—"

"It's not your fault."

"I should've made him go into rehab as soon as I saw signs."

"People need to hit bottom before they're ready to address an addiction."

I shook my head. "Mario needed me to look out for him, and I fucked up."

"That's not being fair to you. You're not his father."

"You don't get it."

"What are you talking about?"

"Me and Mario don't have anybody. If we don't look out for each other, nobody will."

"You're not alone. I'm here for you."

"I know, but it's different. You should've seen the look on his face. He was scared, and I left him there."

"He's going to be okay. You did the right thing."

I flopped on her couch. "Bev had the same look when we left New Jersey."

Laura sat beside me. "Bev? Who's that?"

"Our foster sister. She was too young to come with us when we ran away. At least that's what we told ourselves."

"Come on, Beck. You're not responsible for everyone—"

"She was a kid, and we left her with that maniac, Bryant."

"Did you keep in touch with her?"

"How the hell was I supposed to do that?"

"Take it easy. I'm just asking about her."

"We couldn't risk trying to contact her. She didn't have a phone. I called the house line a couple of times, but Mrs. Bryant always answered it."

"Maybe you can try and find her now."

"I did a couple of years ago, but we never tracked her down."

"Maybe she got married."

"I hope she's all right. She was the sweetest kid. Fucking Bryant used to terrorize her."

"What do you mean?"

I pointed to the scar behind my ear. "One day, he was hitting her with a belt for having a frigging sandwich. I tried to protect her, and he smacked my head on the table."

"Oh my God, what an animal."

"That's what he was."

"How could someone like that be a foster parent?"

"The system sucks, that's why. Some people care and try, but tons of kids fall through the cracks."

Toby whined.

"When's the last time he went out?"

Laura got up. "This morning. I'll take him out."

"I'll go too."

Toby tugged the leash and we headed to the stairs. I pointed. "Who's that?"

"I don't know."

A man in a hoodie was looking in the window of my car. "Hey! What the hell do you want?"

The man took off, jumping into what looked like a Toyota. I took the stairs two at a time, hitting the landing as the car screeched out of the lot.

"Who was that?"

I had an idea of who it was but said, "I don't know. Probably just some junkie, uh, punk looking to see if there was anything worth stealing."

"This is a safe neighborhood. We don't have any crime here."

"Maybe the guy was on drugs . . . or who knows."

I hadn't been able to read the plate. All I had was the car was a white, late-model Toyota. There had to be fifty thousand of them in Southwest Florida. It'd be crazy to try and track it down.

Was it Mallory? The guy didn't move like he was a younger man, and they both had medium builds.

"Beck?"

"Oh, sorry."

"What are you thinking about?"

"Nothing."

"You think that man could be the one who set your house on fire?"

The FBI could use her. "No, I'm just trying to process all this."

"How do you know it wasn't him? He could have followed you here."

"I would've picked up on someone tailing me."

"You were upset about Mario. You had to be distracted."

Forget the FBI, Laura could make a killing as a fortune teller. I shrugged and led Toby to a patch of grass. "Come on, boy, do your business."

"Don't you think we should report it to the police?"

"Nothing happened. Just some, uh, guy looking in my window. Just to be safe, make sure you park your car by a light."

"I always try to get a spot by one."

"Good. I'm starving. Why don't you go back upstairs and get lunch ready."

"All I have to do is heat it up."

"My stomach is grumbling. Go ahead, I'll be back up in five."

Laura headed back to her apartment, and I walked Toby in back of the Starbucks. As Toby sniffed for a spot to do his business, I called Detective Moreno.

"Yo, Moe. You have a minute?"

"Sure. What's up?"

I told him about the man looking in my car.

"It could be nothing. Just a punk looking to see if there was something to steal."

"I know, but there was this guy, Mallory, I had a couple of run-ins with him when I was in Delaware."

"That was a long time ago."

"It was, but the man I saw looked like him. Can you check to see if he owns a white Toyota?"

"He lives in Delaware?"

I wasn't sure he was still there. "He did."

"Send me what you have on him, and I'll see what I can find out."

40

Laura slipped her arm around mine as we entered the Flamingo Beach section of the Wonder Gardens.

She said, "Wow, real pink flamingos."

"It's cool, right?"

"It sure is. I can't believe I never came here before."

"They have some nice exhibits."

"It feels like a tropical zoo."

"I like the macaw section, but this Flamingo Lagoon is nice; it has that old-Florida feel to it."

"Why do you think God made these flamingos pink?"

"I don't know that God did it. It seems more likely the result of evolution. Maybe the pink color helped camouflage them from predators."

"I like to think God put pretty things on earth for us to enjoy."

Along with a ton of dangerous people? "Maybe." My cell rang. "I got to get this."

I stepped away. "Hey, Moe. What's happening?"

"I checked the national registry of titles, Mallory isn't listed—"

"Damn it!"

"It was a long shot."

"It looked like him."

"You haven't seen him in years."

"Trust me, I'll never forget that bastard as long as I live."

"You think of anything else, let me know. I got to run."

"Thanks, Moe."

Laura was kneeling by the lake, trying to coax over a flamingo. She stood. "Everything all right?"

"Yeah, it's all good."

"That was your detective friend, right?"

"Uh-huh."

"What did he want?"

"Nothing."

"Then why'd he call?"

It was easier telling her than being interrogated. "He checked on the car to see if it belonged to someone, but it didn't."

"Who did you think it was?"

"Somebody we worked the other side of a case on."

"What kind of case?"

"Laura, it doesn't matter. Okay? It's not him, and there's no reason to talk about it."

Her mouth tightened.

"Sorry. It was ten years ago, a guy we put away for beating his wife, okay?"

"Oh my God. What a creep."

"I'm dying of thirst. Let's grab some waters."

It was tough pretending I enjoyed the afternoon. Someone was gunning for me, and I was running out of suspects. Would time run out first?

41

THE NEXT MORNING I PULLED INTO PUBLIX'S PARKING LOT.
There'd been less than a quarter of an inch of milk left. Passing
through the grocer's sliders, my cell rang. It was Detective
Moreno.

"Hey, Moe."

"Can you talk?"

I turned around. "Give me a second to step outside . . .
What's up?"

"I did some further checking into Mallory."

"You did?"

"Yeah, something in the way you said you'd never forget
him made me dig deeper."

"What? What did I say?"

"When you were hanging up the other day, you said you'd
never forget him as long as you lived. That reminded me of
what you said about Mallory swearing to get back at you if it
was the last thing he did."

"That's what he said. What did you dig up?"

"I did an address search, and a white Mazda is registered to
a Jill Cashman at Mallory's address."

"How current is the info? Maybe Mallory moved?"

"According to his DMV record, he's still there."

"I don't know, a Mazda? It looked like a Toyota to me."

"Are you sure? Their logos are very similar."

"What model Mazda?"

"A Mazda 3. It's a sedan. Is that what you saw?"

"Yes. Give me a second, I want to pull up a picture. What year does that lady have?"

"2020."

Going to the images tab, I tapped in the model and year. I scrolled to a white auto and zoomed in. The logo on the trunk was close to the one Toyota used. Closing my eyes, I tried to recall the car in Laura's parking lot. It was hard to be sure.

"You know, I could have gotten the vehicle make wrong. It kind of looks like a Mazda, but I can't be sure."

"Delaware has a bunch of special license plates. Some of them look like the ones we have in Florida."

"The one I saw was definitely blue."

"Florida has several blue ones."

Forgetting about groceries, I made a beeline to my car, saying, "Let me call you back, I want to check something."

Regularly looking in the rearview mirror, I drove to Laura's apartment. I tooled around the lot looking for the car I saw. It wasn't there. I parked and hustled to Laura's door.

"Beck? What are you . . . is everything all right?"

I nodded. "I need you to a look at something. See if it looks like the car we saw in your parking lot."

"You found the car?"

I handed her my phone. "No. This is just a generic picture."

She brought the phone closer to her face. "This looks like the car, don't you think?"

"You're sure?"

"Yes. Why? What's going on? You know who it belongs to?"

"Not really."

"So, you came here to show me this, and it doesn't mean anything? I'm not a dummy, you know."

"I didn't say that, it's just confusing and . . ."

"There you go again, right into your turtle shell. You want my help identifying the car but won't tell me anything about whose it is."

"I don't want to scare you. We're not sure about anything. At this point, it's a maybe."

Hands on hips, she demanded, "Tell me."

"Okay, okay. Remember the guy Mallory, in Delaware, I told you about?"

"The man you stabbed?"

I nodded. "He deserved it. It was self-defense. I mean, the bastard bashed my head with a stick, and I just reacted."

"It's him?"

"It could be. A woman named Jill Cashman lives at the same address he does and owns a Mazda like the one we saw."

"Can't the police do something?"

"We don't even know if it was him, and if it was, all he was doing was looking in my car."

"The guy tried to kill you, for God's sake. He set your house on fire."

"Take it easy. We can't pin it on him."

"You're just going to wait around for him to try—"

I took her hands. "Come on, you know me better than that. Trust me, I'm on guard, and we're keeping an eye on him."

It was another picture-perfect day, but I was cooped up inside trying to stay safer. I looked through the sliders, checking the lanai. Nothing but sunshine, the lake, and lush greenery.

The feeling that something needed doing kept nagging me. If it was Mallory, I was prepared. And Detective Moreno had put out a bulletin advising the Collier County Sheriff's Office to look out for Mallory and the Mazda.

What was off? Pacing the family room, I realized it was Mario. In the thirty-plus years we'd known each other, never had a day gone by without us talking to each other. Even when we argued, we always did a quick touch-base. Neither of us had parents or siblings to connect with, just each other.

Laura was good, maybe great, and it was either she or Mallory that kept my mind off my brother from another mother. But nobody could replace Mario. Nobody understood the bond we'd formed.

I dialed the number for Celadon Recovery and asked for Paul.

"Hey Paul, it's Beck. I wanted to check up on Mario. How is he doing?"

"Mario is doing good and appears to be adjusting well. I'm told he seems ready to do the work he needs to do."

"Great. That's good to hear. When can I visit him?"

"We'll let you know. Don't take another trip up here until we advise you it's time."

"Another trip? What do you mean?"

"I was informed someone came this morning. I assumed it was you."

"No. Who was it?"

"I don't know."

"Look, this could be serious. I need you to find out who it was."

"I don't know—"

"Don't visitors have to show identification?"

"Yes, it's required, but only when an actual visit takes place."

"I need to see the security footage."

"What's going on? Is there a threat we should know about?"

"There's nothing to worry about. Let me see the surveillance video just to be sure."

"I can't authorize something like that. Only the director has that ability."

"Check with him. I'm on my way."

42

———

Stuck in a line of traffic leading to Bonita Beach Road, I made a call.

"Detective Moreno."

"Hey, Moe. I need you to meet me at Celadon, in Fort Myers."

"The rehab place?"

"Yeah. Mario is drying out there."

"What's going on?"

"I think Mallory or whoever the hell is coming after me went there. I need to see the surveillance footage."

"Why would they go after him?"

"They might, if it's related to what we do."

"But if it's Mallory, you think—"

"I don't know, man."

"How would they know Mario is there?"

"Look, if I had all the answers, I wouldn't be asking for help."

"Take it easy, I'm just trying to figure out what's going on."

"Can you meet me?"

"Sure. I'm on my way."

Tailgating like a guy from New Jersey, I weaved through traffic, flooring it as I passed the Promenade. A pair of landscaping trucks lumbering in the left lanes slowed traffic. I swerved into the right-hand lane and blew past them.

Slowing for a changing light at Coconut Point, I pushed the accelerator down and nearly hit a car exiting the mall. A quarter mile away from Corkscrew Road, I saw it. A patrol car, lights blazing, was in my rearview mirror.

I maneuvered into another lane, but the cop slid right behind me. "Shit!"

Badge hanging off his belt, Moreno was in the circular driveway talking to one of Celadon's security guards. I parked under the portico and climbed out of my car. "Sorry, man. I got a frigging ticket."

Moreno chuckled. "Lee County?"

"Yeah."

"Who pulled you over?"

"Officer Leahy."

"I don't know him, but give me the ticket. I'll see if I can persuade him to kill it."

"Thanks."

He introduced me to the guard. "Joe, this is Beck."

We shook hands. "Nice to meet you."

"Can you show us the surveillance video?"

"Sure thing. Let's do it."

He took a card out of his pocket and held it against a reader. The entrance doors slid open.

The receptionist perked up. Joe said, "They're with me."

We followed him into a small room. A guard was sitting at a

desk covered in monitors. "These gentlemen need to see the entrance footage from this morning."

"Sure, what time frame?"

I said, "Starting at nine, if that's okay?"

"Shouldn't be too hard to find what you're looking for, it was a quiet morning." He tapped on a keyboard. "Okay." He pointed to a second-tier monitor. "It's on this one."

Joe said, "Why don't you take a break. I'll keep my eye on things."

"Sure, I'll be out back. Text me when you're done."

He squeezed his way out of the room, and Joe sat in his chair. Finger poised over the mouse, he said, "Ready?"

"Do it."

Moreno said, "That's a good camera system."

I said, "I hope it helps. Fast-forward until there's action."

At nine twenty a van pulled up. My shoulders tensed. "Slow it down."

"It's just the laundry guys."

A man appeared, carrying two large, clear plastic bags full of folded linens. He hit the intercom and waited for the doors to open. He disappeared inside, returning with three bags, which he tossed into the van.

At nine fifty-eight a man came into view. "Slow it down." I leaned in as the recording switched to normal speed. He stepped off the driveway and went toward the entrance.

"Pause it and zoom in."

Inches away from the screen, I turned to Moreno. "It's not Mallory."

"All right. Do you recognize him?"

I studied the man's face. He was in his late thirties with two days' worth of stubble. He was stocky and wearing jeans and a blue T-shirt. I shook my head. "Who the hell is this guy?"

"Should I run the rest?"

"Go ahead."

The mystery man hit the intercom, said something, and looked left and right. He jawed at the speaker and walked away.

Moreno said, "Run it again but in slow motion. We might see something."

It was a good idea, but it didn't help.

I said, "We've got to see if Mario knows who it is, Joe. Can you ask Paul if we can just see him for a minute?"

He picked up the phone and dialed an extension. After a brief chat he hung up. "Paul said he just went into a group session and then he has a one-on-one with Dr. Belcher."

"How long is all that going to take?"

"Two hours."

"Let me talk to Paul."

Joe dialed and handed me the phone. "Hey Paul, I know Mario is going to be tied up, but all I need is a minute to show him the video, see if he knows who it is."

"I'm sorry, but we can't interrupt his therapy. Mario is making progress, and something like this might set him back."

"Aw, come on, he's just going to look at a picture. How the hell is that dangerous?"

"Mario needs to stay focused on himself and his recovery. It's a delicate process, and we can't take the chance there'll be a setback."

Swallowing my anger, I said, "When can we see him?"

"In another week."

"Okay. Look, I'm being overly cautious here, but there is a chance someone might be after Mario."

"After him? For what reason?"

"I don't know, but there have been some strange things happening, and we have to be sure to protect him."

"Of course."

"Can you make sure I'm the first to see him?"

"Hmm, that choice is up to Mario."

"Look, we both want what is best for Mario, and the two of us are brothers from another mother. There's a small chance he's in danger, so I really need you to make an exception."

"I'm sorry, but we can't make exceptions."

43

———

Pulling into Celadon's employee parking lot, I shut my headlights. I waited a minute and sent a text. Keeping an eye on the entrance, I climbed out of my BMW.

Under the cover of a gumbo-limbo tree, I checked my phone. A text came in. A couple of the cameras were off. It was time to go.

I jogged to the sliver of light coming from a door and slipped inside a hallway. A second later, Joe appeared. He had a finger to his lips.

I handed him four one-hundred-dollar bills. He stuffed them in his pocket, whispering, "Stay here." He disappeared behind a door marked Locker Room.

Two minutes later, the door swung. A smile erupted on my face. I opened my arms and embraced Mario. "Man, how are you doing?"

"Good. It's the middle of the night, what's going on?"

"Just wanted to show you a picture of someone."

"Who? What's it about?"

"It might be the guy who's after me."

I handed him three photos I'd made from the video footage.

Mario said, "You think Gene is after us?"

"You know him?"

"Yeah, he's Susan's brother."

My shoulders dropped. "Are you shitting me? That's Susan's brother?"

"Yeah, what makes you think he wants to get us?"

"Uh, he came here to try to see you and, I just thought, you know, it could be Mallory. He has the same car as the one I saw by Laura's and, forget it, it's just—"

Mario smiled. "It's just that you're paranoid. I know, it's okay, man." He hugged me. "I appreciate you keeping an eye on me."

"All the time, brother. Are you doing okay?"

"Oh yeah. Haven't felt this good in, like, two years."

"Great. I'm proud of you, man."

Joe stuck his head in the hallway. "Let's go."

We embraced again and went our separate ways.

My heart was beating too fast. I did a series of double inhales and slow exhales to slow it and repeated a core stoic principle: being vigilant and active was the only way to maintain control.

———

I shut the alarm and pulled open the slider. "Come on, boy. Do your business."

Toby pranced onto the lawn and lifted a leg by a bush filled with pink flowers. I took a sip of my coffee before setting it on the table. I pulled out my phone and tapped out a text. Moreno had to know; Mallory was still the number-one suspect.

Toby was circling when my detective buddy Moreno called me back. "Hey, how are you?"

"Good. It turns out the guy who went to see Mario was his girlfriend's brother."

Moreno laughed. "You made me drive to Fort Myers for that?"

"Sorry."

"No big deal. I'm off tomorrow. You want to grab lunch?"

"Sure. Where do you want to go?"

"My neighbor's kid is working at a new place on Vanderbilt that's supposed to be really good."

"Okay. What's it called."

"The Bicyclette Cookshop. Pretty sure it used to be Fit and Fuel."

"Oh yeah, I heard they changed it around."

"They did, and the chef just won some TV-show competition."

"Wow. That's something."

"It's a big deal. Does twelve thirty work?"

"Sure. See you there."

The Pavilion shopping center had changed over the years. After losing a Publix as an anchor and struggling, it morphed into a mix of stores and popular eateries. I grabbed one of Bicyclette's four-foot door handles and pulled it open. A stabbing pain over my right hip froze me in my tracks.

I inhaled deeply and took a step. The pain was still there. I limped into the restaurant.

Moreno was sitting at a table in the rear of the place. "You hurt your leg?"

"It's my back. If you can believe it, I hurt it opening the door."

"It happens to the best of us. You have a spa, right?"

"Yeah, why?"

"Anytime my back starts acting up, I go in the spa. I make it as hot as it gets and point the jets at the area bothering me. It relaxes things and it feels better."

"Really?"

"It works for me, try it."

"I'll give it a shot." I pointed behind him. "That wall is cool." It was covered in slats of wood.

"They used a couple of different woods in here."

I eased into a chair. "It warms things up. I like what they did in here."

He pointed. "You see the bar?"

"Oh yeah. Very nice."

"I ordered an appetizer to get us started. My neighbor said not to miss the chorizo potatoes."

I picked up the menu. "Sounds good."

"How's Mario doing?"

"I only saw him for a second last night, but he seemed good."

"When can he have visitors?"

"Another few days, but he can get calls starting tomorrow."

The server brought the appetizer over. I ordered a tuna burger and Moreno asked for a whitefish dish.

Moreno stabbed a potato. "So, it wasn't Mallory after all."

"It could still be him."

"These are good. Have some."

I ate a piece. "I like it. It has a little kick."

The server set our meals down.

"There's some kinda spice in the sauce. Other than Mallory, you've had some, shall we say, interesting cases. Is there anybody from them you think it could be?"

"I gave it a ton of thought. Yeah, I mean, we evened a

bunch of scores, but they all deserved it. Besides, we keep a low profile."

"But that business with Royal got you some press."

I cut a wedge out of my burger. "Thanks for the reminder."

"Royal is as dangerous as they get."

"Again, don't need the reminder." I stuffed the piece in my mouth. "I think they use the same kind of sauce on this."

"It's probably the spice."

"How's that?"

"Excellent. It's smoked with a bit of jalapeno."

We finished our lunch, and the server cleared the table. "Can I interest you in the dessert menu? We have—"

I said, "Not me, thanks."

Moreno said, "Just the check, please."

He pulled the bill out of his apron and both of us put our Sapphire credit cards down.

My back felt pretty good driving home, but getting out of the car a sharp pain ran across the lower part. I'd try what Moreno said helped. I went into my bedroom to change into a bathing suit.

Emptying my pockets into a drawer, I sighed, "Damn."

I had Moreno's credit card, and he had mine.

Moreno responded to my text, saying he was on the way to a Port Charlotte hospital to visit an aunt. Then he had a pickle-ball lesson and a match. He'd stop by in the evening and would send a text when he was on the way.

I eased myself into the spa. My skin burned. Sitting, I slid over and directed two nozzles at my lower back. After five minutes I moved around. The pain was almost gone.

Moreno was onto something. After twenty minutes I got out and dried off. I felt ninety percent better. I headed inside to do some paperwork.

After eating a can of Costco's chicken for dinner, I laid on the floor, gently stretching my legs and back. The pain began to flare up. Sitting in the spa worked. I'd go back in.

Stretching my hamstring, a text pinged: Moreno would be here in five minutes.

I rolled onto my knees and slowly got up. Toby was standing by his bowl. I'd forgotten to feed him. I filled his dish with food and went outside to turn the heat on in the spa. After getting my credit card back, I'd soak in the water.

After flicking the button on, I put my hands on a column and put my left leg further behind. Stretching my calf and hamstring felt good. I changed legs.

Bending at the hip, I let my arms down but didn't try to touch the ground. The *thwack* of a branch jolted me upright. Toby was curled up in his bed in the kitchen.

The water circulating was the only sound. I dipped my hand in the spa.

"Police! Get your hands up!"

I stiffened.

"Freeze!"

A shot rang out. I crouched behind the spa as a man screamed, "Fuck!"

"Beck! It's Moreno! He's down. Call 9-1-1."

I tore into the house to a side window. Moreno had handcuffed a man in black and was digging in the man's rear pocket.

Dialing 911 with one hand, I grabbed my Glock out of my nightstand and headed outside.

Moreno was tying a tourniquet around the man's thigh. I looked at the injured man's face. "Who the hell is he?"

He handed me his wallet. "Anton Solenko. You know him?"

"No." I knelt. "Who sent you?"

The man closed his eyes. I pressed my Glock under his chin. "Tell me or I'll blow your fucking head off."

Moreno swatted my hand away. "Let me handle this."

The detective pressed his fist on the man's wound.

The man shrieked, "Ow!"

"Who do you work for?"

The man repeated a name. It was the last person I'd thought of.

44

———

Sirens drawing nearer, I said, "Moe, thank God you were here."

"They say timing is everything."

"How did you see him?"

"As soon as I turned onto your block, I saw a sedan, lights off, rolling to a stop close to your house. I cut my lights and pulled over. This guy got out of the car but didn't close the door. He had a ski mask on his head, the kind you can pull down. He looked right at your house and headed between it and the one next door. I figured he was a thief. But when he reached in his belt and pulled out a gun, I hurried my ass over."

"I was on the lanai, getting the spa ready for my back."

A cop car screeched to a halt. Moreno said, "As soon as we take a statement from him, we'll pick up Weiss."

"I still can't believe it was Weiss who hired him."

"Did you forget? You blew up his world, man. And the dude has endless resources."

We watched an ambulance slide to a stop. "Come on, I've put other people in jail. Weiss got what he deserved."

"I'm not saying the guy didn't deserve it, just that status

meant everything to Weiss, and you knocked him off the top of his mountain."

A WINK news van pulled up. "I better call Laura. She finds out before I tell her . . ."

Moreno smiled. "Smart man. Hurry up, you're going need to give a statement."

Mario's therapy ended at two. I waited until five minutes past and called.

"Hey, Mario. How are you, man?"

"Beck. It's so good to hear your voice."

"I would've called sooner, but they have rules and all."

"I know. I asked, and they told me about them. But it's all good."

"How are you feeling?"

"Good. It gets boring at times, but it's better than I expected. The people here are really nice, and boy, do they know what they're talking about."

"Good therapists?"

"Yeah, I mean, you know, after everything we've been through, it's good to, you know, to dig into some of it."

"I bet it helps."

"It does. You should think about seeing someone. It'll be good for you."

"Maybe one of these days."

"It doesn't pay to wait. It's been building up in you for a long time, bro."

"Enough about me, how are you doing with the, uh, you know, the cocaine?"

"I'm an addict."

I flinched at the word. "No, you're not."

"Yes, I am. I'm done lying to myself."

"The easiest person to bullshit is yourself."

Mario continued, "That's true, but I'm going to be honest with myself from now on. That and the tools they're giving me to deal with the desire, I'll be fine. I can you tell you, bro, there's no way I'm going back to that crap."

"That's great. I'm super glad you nipped this in the bud."

"If it weren't for you, I wouldn't have come to a place like this."

"The important thing is you did."

"Thanks, bro."

"Any time."

"So, what's going on? How are the cases going?"

"Oh, man, you're not going to believe it, but it was Weiss who set my house on fire."

"Weiss? The short seller guy?"

"Yeah, all along I thought it was Mallory or maybe Royal, but it was Weiss. He hired a guy out of Orlando, paid him a hundred grand to try and burn me alive—"

"I bet you he was behind the fire at that aviation factory."

"Me too, but Weiss didn't stop there, the bastard spent another hundred grand to get someone to try and shoot me."

"Shoot you? When?"

I told him how Moreno rolled up and saw the would-be assassin.

"Holy shit, if it wasn't for Moe, you'd be dead."

"I know."

"How does that make you feel?"

Was he putting me on the couch? "I didn't think about it too much."

"Come on, man. It's important to process things like this."

I hesitated. "Well, to be honest. It's got me off balance a little."

"It's normal to be rattled."

"But it's not being rattled. I don't know, but I'm starting to wonder if what we're doing is right, you know? I mean, we're helping people and making good money doing it, but shit, someone tried to kill me."

"It's okay to be scared."

"I'm not scared, it's just confusing."

"You should take a break. Step away now and reflect—"

"I can't take off now, we're in the middle of the Jackson and Kravitz cases. I can't leave them hang—"

"Hey, I'm sorry, but my time is up, I got to go."

After hanging up, I plopped on the couch. The good feeling I had about Mario seeming to have straightened out was clouded by the Weiss fallout. I didn't think I'd gone far enough with Weiss, but he thought I had.

Being focused on people like Whitmore was the right thing. But not accounting for the differences in responses from the people we got revenge on had almost killed me.

45

———

Simone Jackson, in a baseball cap and wearing glasses, kept her head down as she walked into the Immokalee Casino. Though Carl was playing a tournament in Miami, Jackson wanted to keep as low a profile as possible.

She made a beeline to the cashier and handed over what amounted to her paycheck. Jackson's stomach was queasy as she walked across the casino floor. She told herself it was going to be a good night.

She breezed past the seven-card stud and Omaha Hi-Lo tables to the section reserved for Texas Hold'em. She watched the play at two tables before moving to a third one.

Jackson felt her confidence rise as she studied the players. There were four of them: a woman she believed was in her early thirties, and three men, all of them in the forty- to fifty-year-old range.

A man seated to the right of the woman had so many piercings it looked as if he'd fallen into a tackle box. To his right was a male with a shaved head, and the last player was bearded.

Though the female was unattractive, she thought the males

would vie for the woman's attention. Jackson swiveled the stool next to her and put her chips on the green felted table.

She smiled at the young woman, who nodded. Mr. Shaved Head said, "I hope you're going to change my luck."

"I'll try my best."

The dealer dealt out the hole cards. The preflop bet came to Jackson. Rather than risk fifty dollars, she folded. She kept her eyes on the men, watching what they did as they played.

The hand unfolded quickly, and it was time for the final community card to be revealed.

The dealer turned the river card over, and the bald man winked at Jackson. He shoved a small stack of chips into the pot. "Five hundred."

The rest of the players bowed out. The man with the piercings said, "What did you have?"

Baldy raked in the pot. "You got to pay to see, my friend."

"You had a flush."

"If that's what you think."

The next round was dealt. Jackson drew the cards to her chest and looked at them. She set them down. A three and an eight, unsuited, weren't playable. She felt good discarding her cards; she was playing smart.

The next hand was passed around. She evened the hole cards and looked at the bottom one, a ten of diamonds. A decent card. Jackson squeezed out the next one, a nine of diamonds. It was her turn to make the preflop bet. She called the bet, adding her fifty dollars to the pot.

The dealer revealed the flop: an ace of clubs, a king of clubs, and a seven of hearts. Jackson checked, but the next player pushed in two black chips. She figured he had a pair of aces or kings. When the bet came around, she folded.

She dropped out before the flop on the next hand, but on the following hand she had a pocket pair of jacks. She called the preflop bet of fifty dollars. The next player raised it to a hundred. Every player stood in. Jackson liked her hand, but somebody could have aces, kings, or queens.

The dealer turned over the flop, a jack of spades, a ten of spades, and a four of hearts.

With three of a kind, Jackson waited for the bet to come to her. She raised the two-hundred-dollar bet to three hundred. Two players matched it.

The turn card was revealed. Another jack, this time in hearts. Jackson told herself to be steady. She had four of a kind. It was a great hand that came around only once every four thousand hands.

The shaved-headed man bet four hundred, then the next player bowed out. Jackson took her time, pushing in chips. "Raise it to five hundred."

Baldy reraised her. "Let's make it six hundred."

Jackson pressed her hands onto the table to keep them from shaking. "Okay, I'm in." She added another black chip to the pot.

The river card was revealed, a queen of spades. The man checked. Jackson studied the community cards. Maybe he was hoping for a royal flush and didn't get it. If he had a strong hand, he would have bet.

Jackson pushed chips in. "Five hundred."

"A thousand."

Jackson was trapped. Was it a bluff? Or had he drawn her in? She estimated the pot to be at least three thousand dollars. At six to one or more, it was favorable. She put five more chips in.

Baldy smiled. "Lady, you've been good to me." He turned over his cards. He had a straight flush. It was a rarity, coming around once every seventy thousand hands.

Bile splashed the back of Jackson's throat. Jackson had lost half her money.

Preflop, she dropped out of five straight hands. She steadied herself, reminding herself that she had played the four-of-a-kind hand well, and that Carl had said that even with the highest odds of winning in your favor, you could lose. He'd said luck wasn't how pros played, but sometimes bad luck would upset your plans.

Baldy was talking to the dealer, and Jackson realized she hadn't been watching the players.

Jackson brightened when she peeked at her hole cards, a pair of kings. She was cautious when it was her turn, calling the one-hundred-dollar bet.

The flop was perfect, a pair of sixes and another king. She had a full house. The man with the piercings bet four hundred. The younger lady upped it to five hundred.

Jackson wanted to raise but didn't want to scare anyone out. She pushed in five black chips.

The dealer turned over the turn card. The fourth community card was a nine of diamonds. The man bet five hundred. The girl dropped out.

Jackson held her breath. When she exhaled, she said, "All in." She counted how much she had in front of her. Thirteen hundred and twenty-five dollars' worth of chips.

The man looked at her before saying, "Call." He put in eight hundred and twenty-five dollars.

The river card was a three of clubs.

The dealer nodded, and Jackson and the man turned over their cards. "Jesus Christ!" Jackson got up and walked away. Her full house lost to the guy's four sixes.

Throat closing like a vise, she stormed into the parking lot. She had lost all her money. And she had played smartly, with restraint.

Jackson turned onto Immokalee Road, replaying the two

exceptional hands she felt certain were winners. Nothing jumped out as a mistake.

She wasn't a pro but had improved and couldn't think of any way Carl would've played the hands differently.

As frustrating as it was, Jackson told herself it was just bad luck. If she kept learning and playing with discipline, she'd win.

46

―――――――

JACKSON WAS STANDING ON THE ELEVATED SIDEWALK OUTSIDE of Brick Coffee and Bar. Carl skipped up the steps. "Let's grab a coffee."

They entered the small shop and waited in line. Jackson said, "You come here often?"

"A couple of times a month. Not too many places serve Lavazza coffee."

"It sure is busy."

"Tourists love this place. Not only is it on Fifth Ave., but a lot of travel sites have it as a favorite that won't break the bank."

"The sandwiches look good."

"I like their paninis, especially the Italian one. You should get one, you're too skinny."

"I'm not hungry."

Carl pointed outside. "What kind of coffee do you want?"

"Just a regular."

"Okay." He pointed. "Grab that table before someone else does."

Jackson sat at one of the three outdoor tables squeezed onto the sidewalk. Minutes later, Carl weaved through a throng of passersby and set their coffees down.

He sipped his coffee. "I don't know why espresso never caught on in the States."

"It's too strong."

"The Italians call American coffee, soup."

Jackson smiled. "One time I had Turkish coffee, it's thick and gritty."

"Exactly, it's sandy. You ready to get down to business?"

"Here? It's so busy."

"So is a casino. Do you know the Italians use the word casino to describe a mess or a confusing situation?"

"Hmm."

"You have to be able to focus, block out everything around you, if you're going to win at the poker table."

"You know, you're right, teach." She smiled.

Carl drained the last of his java. "Okay, class is in session. It's after the flop. You have two pairs. What is the chance of improving the hand to a full house?"

Jackson blinked. "Uh, around ten percent, maybe more."

"It's nine, but that's good. What about drawing an inside straight?"

"Oh, that's the same as getting a full house."

"Very good. Okay, let's say your pocket cards are a jack and eight of spades. The flop has a nine of spades, ten of hearts, and a jack of clubs. For a straight you need a queen or a seven to drop."

"That gives me eight outs, four for the queen and four for a seven. A pretty good hand."

"Maybe, you have to look at what happens if a queen drops because the board will then show a nine, ten, jack, and queen. That means anyone with a king has a king-high straight beating your queen-high one."

"So, I'd need a seven."

"Exactly. Now, somebody might not be holding a king, but in a big game it's a scary position to be in."

"Would you fold?"

"Depends on what the bet is and what the pot looks like."

"That makes sense."

"You're doing good, learning quicker than I expected."

"Thanks."

"Calculating pot odds with consideration of your hand is the next step. I'll simplify it as best I can."

A car with an annoying baffle sound passed by as she said, "Okay."

"Let's say you have a three and a four of hearts as hole cards. No one bets preflop, so you stay in. The flop is a two, a five, and a nine, none of them hearts. Someone bets seven dollars into a thirty-dollar pot. Do you call?"

"I'd say so."

"Don't say so—calculate the pot odds and make a decision."

"Okay."

"The pot odds are the seven dollars into the forty-four-dollar pot."

"Forty-four? It was a thirty-dollar pot."

"The original thirty plus the seven bet and your call of seven."

"Got it."

"So that's about sixteen percent."

"Okay."

"So that means we need to win at least sixteen percent of the time to break even. So, let's figure out our chances of making the straight. We have eight outs in an open-ended straight, meaning we'll make it on the turn sixteen percent of the time. That meets our minimum, plus we have the river card coming as well. This is a profitable call to make."

Jackson stared blankly.

Carl smiled. "Your eyes are glazed over." He leaned forward. "I know it's confusing. It's going to take time to ingrain the math. Believe me, if you stick with it, it'll be automatic after a while."

Jackson exhaled. "I know, but I'm anxious to play, you know?"

"Of course. Look, you can start soon. There's a tournament coming up, and from what I hear, a lot of the heavies are going to be in Vegas, so the competition is lighter. It'd be a good place to wet your feet, and you'll probably finish in the money."

"When is it?"

"In about two weeks. It'll give you some more time to work on pot odds. I will give you the details on it."

"I can't wait." Her smile crumpled. "How much is the entrance fee?"

"Five thousand."

"Oh, that's high."

"Higher than many, but the return is among the best out there."

Jackson was silent.

"Is it too much for you?"

"No. I just have to move some things around."

"Good. But don't wait too long; the fee has to be paid a week before play starts."

47

———

A CROWD ERUPTED INTO A CELEBRATION. JACKSON TURNED toward her right, where people around a craps table were high-fiving each other. She wondered what point the shooter made.

She turned her attention back to the Texas Hold'em table Carl was seated at. He was slowly building stacks of chips. Jackson thought about the difference in his approach to gambling.

Craps players were the most demonstrative players in a casino. Carl was quiet, measured, and methodical. Were those the traits of a winner, or did the emotional ups and downs have to be avoided so as not to burn out a regular player?

A cocktail waitress took orders from the players at Carl's table. Jackson wanted a drink and checked her purse: a couple of singles and two twenties. Cheering from a roulette table drew her attention.

Roulette paid thirty-five to one. Twenty bucks would return seven hundred if her number came up. She could take two shots. The odds would still be terrible. What if Carl found out? Would he let it pass, or would he stop mentoring her?

A text pinged in. Jackson pulled her phone out. It was an

email from Summit Mortgage Corporation. She hesitated before opening it:

Dear Ms. Jackson,

We regretfully decline your application for a loan against 1123 Palmetto Drive due to a lack of equity.

You may resubmit an application using another property as equity . . . blah-blah-blah.

Jackson deleted the message and pinched the bridge of her nose. Where else could she borrow from? Maybe she should just sell her house and start over. In a year or two, she'd be a much better player and would buy something else with her winnings.

Jackson forced her attention back to the oval table Carl was playing at. She shut out the hum of whispered conversations and chiming slot machines and focused on the game. The bet was to a hip-looking woman in her late thirties who was studying her cards with intensity.

Jackson tried to determine if she was bluffing to hide a strong hand or was really trying to make a decision. The woman put her fingers around a stack of chips. "Call."

Carl's gaze moved from player to player. Jackson knew he had to have a good hand, figuring him for a high pair, maybe kings as hole cards. The four community cards carried the risk of a flush and straight possibilities.

The dealer flicked over the river card, a ten of hearts. The woman's eye ticked. Had she gotten the flush? The bet was to Carl, who checked.

Wearing a yellow soccer shirt, the next player shoved his pile of chips in and stood. "All in."

The two players to his left folded as the dealer counted out the bet Mr. Soccer had made. "Fourteen hundred and fifty."

The bet was to the woman. She looked at her hole cards.

Jackson knew it was nerves; the woman hadn't forgotten what she held. Jackson figured the woman would bow out.

The woman slid her cards toward the dealer. "Out."

Jackson smiled and held her breath as Carl looked at the standing man and moved three stacks toward the center. "I'm calling."

Jackson saw Mr. Soccer stiffen as Carl turned over his cards. "Three jacks."

"You beat me, man."

Carl raked in the pot as the loser walked away.

After a dozen more hands, Carl asked for a color change. He tipped the dealer and stuffed his pockets with chips.

Jackson held up a palm. "Sweet playing." Carl didn't high-five her.

"Win or lose, never call attention to yourself. It's not fair to the players you beat, and you sure as hell don't want the casino watching you any more than they already do."

"Okay, sorry."

"No problem."

"You had me nervous there on that all-in pot. How did you know he didn't have the flush?"

"I wasn't certain, but the pot odds were excellent, and when he stood, to me, it screamed a bluff. If you had the flush, what was there to be nervous about? There wasn't a pair on the board, so the best hand was either a straight or three of a kind."

"Yeah, you're right. You really know this game."

"It's not a game, it's a combination of understanding behaviors with a ton of math thrown in."

"You make it sound easy."

He shook his head. "Trust me, it's not easy. But if you put the work in and have discipline, you'll have a good shot at winning consistently."

"I'm doing the work."

"I know you are."

"By the way, I knew that woman was going to bail."

"What tipped you off?"

"She kept looking at her cards. And when the river came out, she had a tick in her eye."

"Good observation. How are you doing with the pot odds?"

"It's not easy, but I'm working through a workbook I downloaded."

"The one from Split Suit?"

"Yes."

"Stick with it and you'll get there."

"When do you think I should play?"

"I told you about that tournament. I think you're good enough to play. Why don't you register?"

"Okay, I will."

"Don't forget our agreement. Whatever you win, I get a piece."

"Believe me, I'll be happy to pay your share."

"I have to run. My girlfriend is flying into Fort Myers in a little over an hour."

"Get going then."

They stepped out into the parking lot and split up. Jackson headed to her car feeling good about what Carl said about her progress.

She tried to replay the conversation. When she got to the end regarding his cut, he'd said 'whatever you win.' She smiled; it wasn't 'if' she won.

Jackson visualized sweeping a large pot of chips in. Her face broke out into a smile. But her high deflated—she didn't have the money to pay the entrance fee.

48

Jackson told herself things would work out as she stepped into the Immokalee Casino. She hesitated before meeting up with Carl. She had a few minutes. Should she put the hundred she borrowed from a coworker down on the roulette wheel?

It was one of the longest shots, but she was overdue. Jackson peeked into the Lucky Mi Bar.

Carl was sitting on a stool talking to the bartender. The barman threw a chin toward the rows of slot machines just outside the lounge. Carl swiveled his chair and smiled at an approaching Jackson.

"Hey, how are you?"

"All right."

"What do you want to drink?"

She slid onto a stool. "A club soda."

The bartender filled a glass, set it on a coaster, and went to serve another customer.

Carl said, "Are you feeling all right?"

Jackson said, "I'm okay."

"Are you sure? You don't look right."

"What are you talking about?"

"Your shoulders are droopy and you're much quieter than usual."

"What, do you analyze everyone? Even when you're not playing against them?"

Carl shrugged. "It comes naturally."

She sucked on her straw before saying, "It might be the cigarette smoke. I can't stand the smell of it. Why don't they do something about it?"

"You never mentioned anything about it before."

"Well, it's getting to me today."

"You got to shut it out."

"Sometimes it's easier said than done."

"Cheer up, will you?"

She nodded.

"How are you doing with the pot odds workbook?"

"I don't have it all, but I feel like it's starting to make sense."

"Good. Keep at it."

"Believe me, I'm going to."

Carl smiled. "I have to admit, I gave you a fifty-fifty shot of sticking with it. I'm glad you proved me wrong."

"Wow, I beat you at something."

"Well done. Hey, did you register for the tournament?"

She silently shook her head.

"What are you waiting for?"

She shrugged.

"Don't tell me you're afraid. You'll do fine."

"It's not that."

"Then, what's going on?"

Jackson exhaled. "I had a bunch of maintenance to do on the house and it set me back."

"You don't have the money?"

She sighed. "I don't. I'm sick about it, I really want to play."

"That's too bad."

"Tell me about it. I wish there was a way I could get the money."

"You know, there might be something. Let me check with a friend of mine."

"He'd stake me? But that wouldn't be fair to you."

"No, it's something different."

"That would be amazing."

"We don't have much time. Let me see if he can meet with you later tonight or tomorrow morning."

"Okay, let me know."

"You're working tomorrow?"

"Yes."

"If it can't be tonight, I'll see if he can meet you there or somewhere close by."

"Who is this guy?"

"A friend of a friend. He's helped out in a couple of situations."

"Why does he help people he doesn't know?"

"He gets what he wants, and they get what they need."

"What does he want?"

"He'll have to tell you that. I just make the introductions."

49

———————

Jackson looked at the clock on the wall; it was 11:35 a.m. Where was Carl's friend? She tapped out a text to Carl: *Your friend hasn't come. Is he still coming?*

Staring at her screen, the intercom squawked, "Simone, there's a Paul Smith here to see you."

She jumped up. "I'll be right there."

Jackson smoothed her blouse and patted her hair. She grabbed her pocketbook and closed the door to her office behind her.

She stepped into The Florida Department of Children and Families' lobby. Legs crossed, Paul Smith was the only male in the space. "Mr. Smith?"

Smith looked up from his phone and smiled. "That would be me." Standing, he slipped his phone into his jacket. His watch looked expensive. He adjusted his man purse and extended a hand. "Ms. Jackson. It's nice to meet you. Carl told me a lot about you."

"I hope it was all good."

"It sure was. He thinks highly of you."

"He's a very nice person. And smart as they come."

"He is something, isn't he?"

"One of a kind."

Smith lowered his voice. "Carl said I might be able to help."

"Uh, I was just going downstairs to get a coffee. Why don't we grab one together?"

"Sounds good."

Jackson and Smith took the stairs and walked into the sunshine. The whiz of cars traveling over Route 41's speed limit competed with Smith's voice.

Jackson put up a hand. "Hang on until we get there."

They crossed the street into a shopping center housing a Starbucks. They small-talked while waiting for their coffees. Cups in hand, Jackson said, "They have seating out back."

The rear entrance led to an empty terrace dotted with tables and umbrellas. Jackson led Smith to a secluded spot. They pulled up chairs. Smith took off his cross-body man bag and set it on the table. They sipped their coffees.

Jackson said, "Thanks for coming to see me on such a short notice."

Smith put his cup down. "No worries, Ms. Jackson."

"Call me Simone, please."

"So, Simone, I understand you're under a bit of financial strain."

"It's a rough patch, I, uh, had a lot of work done on the house, and that was after a bunch of dental work."

"My friend said the dentists in Naples didn't go to dental school, they went to business school."

Jackson scoffed. "Not far from the truth."

"How much do you need?"

"Five thousand."

"No worries."

"Really?"

"Yes." He looked around and took an envelope out of his

jacket. "There's six thousand in here." He spread open the top, revealing an inch of hundred-dollar bills.

Jackson's eyes widened.

"It's yours. All you need to do is send a couple of kids to the Alliance."

"I don't understand."

"You know there aren't enough foster families to take all the kids in. The Alliance just expanded and has empty beds. You send three kids, preferably under ten years of age."

"What you're asking—"

"Your position gives you the authority, doesn't it?"

"Yes, but—"

He tapped the envelope on the table. "If you want this, you'll do it. If not, I'm on my way." Smith scraped his chair back.

"Hold on a minute. I, uh, have to think this over."

"Don't forget, these kids have to be placed somewhere, and the new edition the Alliance put on is really nice."

"Who do you work for?"

"I freelance for a lot of organizations."

"For the Alliance?"

"Do you want the money or not?"

"Yes."

"And you're going to send the kids?"

"Yes."

"Good." He slid the money across the table.

Jackson snatched it, jamming the envelope into her purse.

"You'll need to send one, if not two, over today."

"Today? That's impossible—"

"Where do you think that money comes from? The per diem rate the state pays is lower than low. The Alliance needs a long stretch of time to make it back."

"Okay, okay. I'll see what I can do."

Smith stood, picking up his man bag. "Nice doing business with you."

A chill crept down Jackson's spine as Smith walked away. When he was out of sight, she opened her pocketbook and put the envelope on her lap. Her heart pounded as she fanned the bills. She stuffed the money back in her purse, stepped to the edge of the terrace, and made a call.

"Carl, I just, uh, met with Paul Smith."

"How did it go?"

"Okay, I guess."

"He gave you the money for the entrance fee?"

"Yeah, but he wants me to do something that could get me fired."

"How so?"

She lowered her voice. "He wants me to send children to the Alliance as they wait for a foster family."

"So? Don't they provide housing for kids in the foster system?"

"Yes, but we don't really have a relationship with them. It'd be—"

"I don't see what the problem is. The kids need somewhere to go, and you're doing that."

"But he's paying, uh, a finder's fee to get me to do it."

"Sounds like a good deal for both parties."

"Can he be trusted to keep it confidential?"

"Yes. Paul is very discreet."

"He better be."

"He will, but make sure you keep up your end of the deal or it could get ugly."

"Ugly? What's that supposed to mean?"

"He's, uh, shall we say, involved with a lot of interesting characters."

"Oh my God, he's in the mob or something? How could you put me in with him?"

"You needed money, who do you think was going to give it to you, an angel?"

"You should have told me—"

"Look, if you do what you agreed to do, you won't have any issues."

"Are you sure?"

"Look, if you want to play the tournament, the registration deadline is five o'clock today."

50

JACKSON TOSSED HER COFFEE INTO THE TRASH AND HURRIED TO her office. She closed the door and pulled open the bottom drawer of her desk.

She grabbed a stack of files, stuck her bag in the drawer, flopped into her chair, and opened a folder.

After staring blankly at the case file, she hit the intercom button. "Freda, where are today's transfer files."

"You signed off on them this morning."

"I know that. Find them and bring them to me ASAP."

"But—"

"I said find them and bring them to me!"

"Okay."

Five minutes later there was a light knock on the door before it swung open. "Simone, it's Freda. I got those files."

"Give them to me."

Freda handed them to Jackson, who said, "We need to divert a couple of them to the Alliance."

"The Alliance? We ain't used them in ages—"

"A memo came in from Tallahassee, they want to spread things around a little."

"Oh, does Bradley know?"

Jackson glared at Freda. "He doesn't make the decisions; I do."

"Oh, I know, but he does the transport and all."

Jackson sorted through a handful of documents. "He'll do what I say."

"Of course."

Jackson pulled two sheets out, crossed out the receiving facility's name, and penned in the Alliance.

After initialing the changes, she said, "Take these to transport and make sure they're done."

Handing back the folder, she said, "I've got an important appointment outside the office this afternoon. If there's a problem, call my cell."

"Will you be back later?"

"Probably not."

"Okay. See you when I see you."

Freda headed for the door. Jackson said, "Uh, hold on a second."

Freda turned around. "What is it?"

"Uh, let me review the transfer paperwork. I want to be sure it's in order."

"It's fine, I seen it."

"My name is on it. I want to double-check things. I'll drop it on your desk on my way out."

As soon as her assistant left, Jackson flipped open the folder. She paged to the edit she'd made. The handwritten change was too obvious.

She tapped at her keyboard, pulling up the first case, a nine-year-old girl. Jackson made the change to the Alliance and printed the page. She repeated the process for the second child she was diverting.

Jackson signed both orders and replaced the pages. She

stared at the file, considering who might question the change. Would Bradley even look at the paperwork? If he did, or if the driver he handed it off to said something, she'd be questioned.

She ran the place, but if she didn't handle it right, the State of Florida would be all over her. If they did, she had no defense for the move. She sank into her chair. It was too dangerous.

Jackson couldn't go through with it. She'd give the money back and forget about the tournament.

She put her fingers on the keyboard, navigating to the digital files. A text pinged. Jackson grabbed her phone. It was Florida Power and Light; she was delinquent on her electric bill.

She leaned back in her chair. Selling her house would only give her enough to pay off half of her debt. If she were to move, she'd need at least six thousand dollars for the first and last month's rent and the security deposit.

Jackson logged off her computer and took her pocketbook out of the drawer. She scooped the folder off her desk and closed the door behind her.

51

───────

THE COUPLE OF DOZEN SPECTATORS BEHIND THE VELVET ROPES quieted down. The dealer flipped over the river card, a seven of hearts. A collective sigh was released. It didn't fit with any of the community cards.

The two remaining players looked at their hole cards. The one wearing glasses looked at his opponent's chips and moved a stack of his own into the pot. "Five thousand."

"Call."

Both players stood. Whoever won would move on to the final table. The man in glasses flipped over his cards, a pair of kings. With the king from the turn card, he had three of a kind.

The other player threw his head back and sighed, "Ah! You got me, two pairs."

The crowd erupted into applause.

The tournament director, a burly man in a dark suit, approached the winner. "Congratulations, Dutch, you're going to play at the championship table."

The dealer made lines of stacks with the chips Dutch had accumulated.

He counted them and said, "Eighty-seven thousand, four hundred."

Dutch nodded. The dealer loaded the chips onto a Lucite tray and handed them to Dutch. "Good luck, sir."

Dutch took three chips and handed them to the dealer. "These are for you."

The crowd from the now empty table shifted to the championship table, encircling it. The remaining players took seats as Dutch walked over to the final table.

He set his tray down in front of the only free chair, sitting to the right of a woman. He said, "I've seen you around with Carl." He extended his hand. "People call me Dutch."

"Nice to meet you, I'm Simone Jackson."

"Good luck, now."

"You too."

Jackson gazed at his tray, figuring he was close to having the most money. She was somewhere in the middle and feeling good about her chances. The prizes were awarded to the top four players.

Winning would be amazing, but she didn't need to. All she had to do was get into the top four. If she came in fourth, she'd take home twenty thousand. If she snagged third place, she'd win twice that.

Jackson told herself to calm down and scanned the room for Carl. Where was he? She took a deep breath through her nose and exhaled slowly.

Dutch swiveled his head. "All right, let's do it."

The tournament director said, "Is everybody ready to play?"

A chorus of yeses rang out.

"Okay, let's get this final round started."

The audience cheered. Card by card, the dealer swiped cards out of the shoe and dealt the six players their hole cards.

Jackson fumbled picking up her first hand. She held her breath and peeked at the cards.

Her heart sped up; she had a pair of queens. The luck she'd had since the first hand, eight hours ago, was holding up. Jackson waited till the bet came to her and raised it.

Two hours later, the first player to go broke left the table. There were now five players. Jackson was one player away from making twenty thousand dollars. She inhaled deeply. A wave of a hand caught her attention.

She smiled. Carl was here. He gave her a thumbs-up. Her shoulders relaxed. She swept her cards off the green felt and, covering them with her hand, peeked at them. A king and queen of clubs.

The preflop bet was five hundred. When it came to her, she took five black chips off her stack, tossed them into the pot, and called.

The dealer turned over the flop cards: a two of clubs, an eight of clubs, and a jack of spades. The bet was to Dutch.

"Check."

Jackson finished doing the math. She knew Carl would have checked, just like Dutch did. She counted out her bet. "A thousand."

The man to her left, a guy with a ZZ Top-Beard, folded. The next player, a woman wearing a yellow blouse, moved her chips in. "Call."

The bet was to a fiftyish man wearing a cab driver's cap. He cleared his throat but said nothing. He looked around the table before examining his hole cards. He slid his cards to the dealer. "Out."

It was up to Dutch. He wrinkled his nose and said, "Call." After he put his money in the pot, the dealer pulled the turn card out of the shoe.

It was a king of hearts.

Jackson was hoping for a club, but at least she had a pair of kings. If she pulled another pair, only two pairs leading with aces could beat her.

The bet was hers to make. She pushed away the feeling it wasn't enough. "Fifteen hundred."

Yellow Blouse put her money in quickly. Jackson's stomach turned. Dutch flicked his cards to the dealer. "I'm out."

The dealer moved the river card from the shoe to the center of the table and flipped it over. A seven of clubs.

Over the whispering, Jackson could hear blood pulsing in her ears. The bet was to the lady in the canary-colored top. She said, "Check."

Jackson silently counted to five before saying, "Fifteen hundred."

Yellow Blouse inhaled. "I've come this far. I'll call." She pushed her chips in, and Jackson turned over her cards. "Flush."

"I thought so. It's yours." Not revealing what she had, the lady pushed her cards toward the dealer.

Jackson looked up. Carl was smiling. She raked the pot in with trembling hands.

Jackson picked up the new cards in front of her: a six and eight of diamonds. She hoped someone would make a preflop bet. Yellow Blouse said, "Three hundred."

Jackson folded. She eyed her competition. Only Dutch and Cabbie Hat had more chips than she did. She was in third place.

Jackson decided to play it conservatively and wait for Yellow Blouse, who had the least amount of chips, to run out of money.

The flop was revealed and ZZ Top-Beard bet. "Fifteen hundred."

Dutch dropped out. Yellow Blouse looked at her chips and pursed her lips. "All in."

The dealer counted the pile. "Forty-two hundred."

ZZ Top-Beard smiled. "Call."

Yellow Blouse shrugged. Jackson knew she was going to lose. The dealer revealed the turn and river cards. ZZ Top turned over his cards. "Full house, aces over tens."

Another man in a suit waddled over and said to the woman, "You played well today and made it to the final table. That's quite an accomplishment."

Yellow Blouse said, "Thank you."

"We hope you'll be back for the next tournament."

"I will." Canary Blouse walked away.

Jackson suppressed a smile; she was in the money. She scanned the chips in front of the remaining players. How far could she go? Could she really win and walk away with the hundred thousand dollars the champion would get?

52

THEY'D BEEN PLAYING FOR OVER TEN HOURS. THE PLAYERS HAD four fifteen-minute breaks and a forty-minute period to eat. Jackson's lower back was bothering her, but she wasn't tired. Adrenaline was coursing through her body.

Jackson inhaled to a count of six and exhaled slowly. She was on her third round of the breathing routine Carl spoke about when her second hole card was dealt. She took a peek: a six of spades and a two of clubs. Before going out, she'd wait to see if anyone bet before the flop.

The bet was to Dutch, and he flicked in a couple of black chips. "Four hundred."

Jackson slid her cards to the dealer. "I'm out."

The dealer turned over the flop, two queens, one in hearts, the other diamonds, and an ace of diamonds.

Looking at the crowd, Jackson saw Carl tapping on his phone. Her attention went back to the table when ZZ Top-Beard started betting. "Fifteen hundred."

Jackson figured he might have an ace as a hole card, giving him two pairs of high cards.

Cabbie Hat didn't hesitate. He moved two stacks of chips forward. "Three thousand."

Dutch pinched his brow. "Make it four thousand."

ZZ Top tossed more chips in. "I'll call." Cabbie Hat also called. The pot swelled from twelve hundred preflop to over thirteen thousand. Jackson knew someone had the aces, maybe three of them, giving them a full house.

The dealer slid the turn card out of the shoe and flipped it over, a six of hearts. It didn't seem to improve any player's hand.

The bet was to Cabbie Hat. "Check." Jackson figured he was trying to see what the others would do.

Dutch's Adam's apple bobbed. He shoveled his chips forward. "All in."

The dealer counted the mound of chips. "The bet is twenty-three thousand, six hundred."

ZZ Top-Beard took a sip of his drink. He put it down and began counting out his chips. "I'm calling."

Jackson figured Cabbie Hat, who had the smallest number of chips, would fold, but he said, "Me too. I'm in."

The eighty-thousand-dollar pot was the biggest Jackson had ever seen. Jackson didn't care who won; no matter who did, two players would be severely weakened.

As the dealer glided the river card, facedown, to the center of the table, Jackson found herself pulling for Cabbie Hat. If he won, two would have way more chips than the others.

The dealer turned the card over, a two of clubs. The audience let out a collective sigh.

Cabbie Hat was the first to reveal his cards: a full house, three queens over a pair of aces. Jackson knew only a royal flush, a straight flush, or four of a kind could beat his hand.

ZZ Top said, "Shit," and flung his hole cards to the dealer.

Dutch said, "It was nice playing with you guys." He extended his hand and shook hands with the other players.

Jackson couldn't do any worse than third, which meant she had at least forty grand coming to her. She eyed the chips in front of the remaining players. ZZ Top-Beard had a slight edge on her, but she had more than Cabbie Hat.

Two men in suits appeared beside the tournament director. The master of ceremonies shook Dutch's hand. "That was some of the most exciting play of the day."

"It was fun. I wish I could've kept going."

"Congratulations on placing fourth."

"Thanks."

The men in suits unfurled a mock check. "The Immokalee Casino is pleased to present you with this prize for your superb efforts."

The crowd applauded. The director said, "It's a great day's pay!"

"It is nice, but it's taken me years of playing to get here."

"We're glad you participated, and we look forward to seeing you compete in the next one."

"Thanks, it was a blast. I'll definitely be back."

"Great. Now, these good gentlemen will escort you to the cashier, where you'll get the real check."

As Dutch followed the men, the director turned to the table. "We're down to the last three players. Good luck to all of you! Let's play some Texas Hold'em!"

The crowd erupted as Jackson glanced at Carl. He gave her a big smile as the dealer passed out the hole cards. She took a look at hers: a five of hearts, and a nine of diamonds.

As soon as Cabbie Hat made a preflop bet, Jackson folded. As the hand unfolded, she thought about winning the tournament. She was playing well, and the card gods had been generous. Coming in first was within her grasp.

As the turn card was revealed, Jackson realized she'd gotten this far using Carl's methods, but was it enough to win? In every book she'd read and all the tournaments she'd watched on TV, the winner took risks. No one won the big prizes without taking a chance.

As ZZ Top raked in the pot, Jackson realized she'd only bluffed twice the entire day. Maybe it was time for a strategic bluff or two. Carl wouldn't approve, but everybody bluffed, even the world's best players.

Jackson discarded her hole cards when Cabbie Hat made a five-hundred-dollar preflop bet. ZZ Top-Beard saw him, and the flop had a pair of eights and an ace. ZZ Top bet a thousand, and Cabbie Cap saw him.

The turn card was a jack, and Cabbie's bet of two thousand was raised to three by ZZ Top-Beard. Cabbie put an extra thousand in, and the dealer swiped the river card from the shoe.

The bet was to Cabbie Cap. The six of hearts didn't seem to help, but he said, "Two thousand."

"Raise it to four thousand."

Cabbie Cap slapped the felt and flicked his cards to the dealer. "I'm out."

Having lost the last two hands, both on the river, Cabbie Hat was a bit more vulnerable. And whether you believe in momentum or not, he was having a bad stretch.

Carl said the right move when your luck was going ugly was to get up and find another table. He was big into cutting your losses. It made sense, but this was a tournament, you had to play the table you were at.

Jackson also remembered Carl saying not to show mercy. When a player was weak, you had to apply pressure, as they were prone to making more mistakes than usual.

53

———

HOLE CARDS DEALT, JACKSON SQUARED THEM AND TOOK A look—a jack of spades. Using her thumb, she squeezed out the next card. The J in the upper left-hand corner was unmistakable; she had a pair of jacks.

ZZ Top-Beard bet a thousand preflop. Cabbie Cap put his money in. Jackson didn't want to scare anyone into dropping out and pushed a stack of chips in. "I'll call."

The dealer turned over the community cards, a six and four of diamonds and a ten of clubs. The bet was to Cabbie Cap. "A thousand."

Jackson pushed in two stacks. "Two thousand."

ZZ Top-Beard matched the bet, and Cabbie Cap put in another ten black chips. The dealer drew the turn card, the jack of hearts.

Hoping to lure them into betting, Jackson said, "I'll check."

ZZ Top-Beard said, "Two thousand."

As he pushed his chips in, Cabbie Cap said, "Let's make it four thousand."

Jackson waited till all the chips were in. She looked at Cabbie Cap's chips. "How much do you have there?"

The color drained from his face. "Uh, about seventeen thousand."

"Okay. Whatever he has, plus the four thousand already bet."

ZZ Top-Beard said, "I'm out."

Cabbie Cap stared at the community cards. "All right, all in."

The only cards Jackson didn't want on the river were an ace, king, or queen for the chance he was holding a pair of them in his hand or any diamond that would give him an opportunity to make a flush.

Cabbie Cap stood up as the dealer dramatically slid the river card to the center of the table. After a pause, the card was revealed, a seven of clubs.

Jackson exhaled and turned her cards over. "Three jakes."

Cabbie Cap tugged on the brim of his headpiece. "I was afraid of that." He bent over and pushed his cards to the dealer, never showing what he had. Jackson scooped up the pot. Stacking her chips, she looked up. Carl was talking on the phone.

The men in suits and the director returned. "Let's give it up for our third-place finisher!"

The crowd cheered as the men in suits held up a facsimile of a forty-thousand-dollar check. The master of ceremonies congratulated Cabbie Cap and finished by saying, "We're going to take a break in this riveting action, and when we come back, we'll find out who'll be our winner!"

Two uniformed guards roped off the table and stood guard as Jackson and ZZ Top-Beard got up. Jackson smiled at the person standing between her and the hundred-thousand-dollar first-place prize.

She walked toward Carl, who looked at his phone and walked away. "Carl! Carl, hold on."

Carl glanced over his shoulder and, picking up the pace, headed for the slot machine section. Jackson was losing ground and she stopped in her tracks when he walked through the sliders into the parking lot.

Jackson figured Carl had some kind of an emergency. She hoped it wasn't too serious. A woman about her age said, "Hey, you're playing great. You're going to win it!"

"Thanks." She went into the ladies' room and focused on the upcoming play.

ZZ Top-Beard was already seated when Jackson got back to the table. The tournament director held the velvet rope aside, and she slipped into her chair. She checked her stacks. Everything was intact.

Jackson had over eighty thousand dollars in chips. It was more than her competitor had, but the difference wasn't enough to influence the play.

"Ladies and gentlemen, the last two contestants are going to battle head-to-head. The winner takes home the grand prize of one hundred thousand dollars and the bragging rights as the champion of this Texas Hold'em tournament. Let's get the contest underway!"

The crowd cheered and the dealer quickly clapped his hands and flashed his palms. He pulled cards from the shoe and delivered hole cards to the players.

Jackson had an eight and nine of clubs. ZZ Top-Beard checked preflop. Jackson bet five hundred and ZZ Top called.

The flop cards were a jack of diamonds, a four of clubs, and a three of hearts. Jackson checked, and ZZ Top-Beard said, "Three thousand."

Jackson flicked her cards to the dealer, and ZZ Top took the meager pot. She scanned the crowd for Carl. He hadn't returned.

The next hand was dealt, and Jackson peeked at her cards.

Her heart rate increased. She put the pair of queens down. The preflop bet started with her.

"Five hundred."

ZZ Top-Beard quickly raised. "A thousand."

Jackson put in the extra money.

The dealer turned over the community cards, a jack and six of spades and the queen of hearts.

ZZ Top-Beard said, "A thousand."

As soon as he pushed his chips in, Jackson raised him, "Two thousand."

"Five thousand."

Jackson originally figured him for a pair of aces or kings. Now she thought he had three jacks. Unless he bluffed earlier, the chance he was going for a straight or flush didn't line up with what he'd bet. And if he did, her hand was superior.

Jackson considered whether to meet the raise and try to suck another couple of thousand out of him or to bet boldly. It was low risk, but possible the turn or river would be a jack, giving him four of a kind and the winning hand.

Jackson wet her lips. "All in."

"I don't have a much as you do, but I'm all in."

The dealer counted out his chips. "Sixty-nine thousand, seven hundred."

As a murmur rippled through the audience, a trickle of sweat rolled down her forehead. Jackson wiped it away, afraid he had two clubs in his hand and was going for a flush.

She calculated the odds using the two and four method Carl taught her. She inhaled deeply, trying to slow her heart rate. There were thirteen clubs in the deck, two were already in the flop, and if he had two in his hand, that left nine clubs left in the shoe.

Roughly, there was a thirty-six percent chance one would appear on the turn, and then it would drop to eighteen percent with the river card. The voice in her head was screaming it had been stupid to go all in.

As the dealer moved to draw a card, the chatter from the audience quieted. As a cheer broke out from a craps table, the dealer revealed the turn card, a six of diamonds.

Jackson exhaled, her mind's voice repeating, *No clubs, no king, no ace. No clubs, no king, no ace . . .*

Over the dealer's shoulder, she noticed the crowd's attention had shifted toward a handful of men in suits. ZZ Top stood, bringing the attention back to the action.

Thin-lipped, the dealer swept his hand to the shoe and dragged a card to the center of the table. He dramatically turned the last card over.

Jackson exhaled. It was a three of spades. She looked at ZZ Top. He exposed his cards, a pair of aces.

A smile erupted on Jackson's face as she flipped over her cards. "Three ladies."

Instinctively, she reached for the pot. A hand grasped her shoulder. She shook it off and raked the chips in.

An arm in a suit jacket grabbed her wrist. "Hey, get off me." She turned around. Her shoulders crumpled when she saw it.

54

———

What she saw was a badge.

"Simone Jackson, put your hands behind your back. You're under arrest."

A buzz rippled through the audience. The master of ceremonies' mouth was wide open.

Jackson said, "What? Get your hands off me."

"You're under arrest." Two of the detectives grabbed her under her armpits. "Come with us, or we'll have to shackle your legs as well."

"What about my money? I won the tournament! I want my money!"

The director said, "It's okay, uh, don't worry, we'll figure this out."

———

Larson's Pelican Marsh neighborhood was quiet. Large lots meant generous space between the homes on the cul-de-sac he lived on.

Reading glasses perched on his head, Larson opened the door. "You're cutting it close."

I followed him into the family room. "You said he was calling at one thirty."

The lawyer had the glass doors to his lanai open. The mix of warm air took the edge off the air-conditioning. "He is."

"What time is it in Hong Kong?"

"Carl's not in Hong Kong, he's in Macau."

"Oh yeah, that's where all the casinos are."

"They say it's the Asian version of Las Vegas."

"What's the time difference?"

"They're thirteen hours ahead."

I did the math. "So, it's like four thirty in the morning?"

"Exactly."

"I couldn't function at that hour."

"Me either, but Carl is one of those guys who adapts to time changes easily. He told me what he does to acclimate, like getting up hours before he would normally and getting, I think it's white light, when he does."

"Does he take supplements, like melatonin or lavender?"

"No, he doesn't even drink alcohol. One time we were on a Zoom. He was at the Horseshoe Casino down in Mississippi, and his windows were all blacked out. I asked him about it, and he said he does it everywhere he sleeps, says he doesn't even want the light from an alarm clock to interfere with his sleep."

"Carl's the most disciplined person I know."

"I guess the way he moves from casino to casino, he's got to be."

"It's bullshit that casinos can bar someone who wins. I mean, he's not cheating."

"They're privately owned businesses, and, as such, don't need a reason to prevent you from playing."

"It's not fair."

"You know better than most about life not being fair."

"That's for sure. You know, when you first told me about Carl, I thought it was bullshit. I mean, I knew there was math involved in gambling, but I never thought you could make a living from it."

"It's not easy, but there are a couple of thousand people making a good living doing it, and at least one guy, Bill Benter, who became a billionaire gambling."

"Is that the guy that golfer got mixed up with?"

"No. Phil Mickelson was connected to a gambler known as Billy Walters, but it didn't end well. He—"

The laptop sitting on the table chimed, and Carl's face filled the screen. Larson picked up the device and set in on the kitchen counter, saying, "Good morning. Sorry to get you up so early."

"No problem, I'm catching an early flight to Melbourne."

"Australia? They have casinos?"

"Oh yeah. It's the world's biggest gambling country."

"I didn't know that."

"Just under eighty percent of the population gambles at least once a year. That's a third higher than in the States."

Larson said, "That's surprising. Look, we appreciate the wonderful job you did with Jackson. It worked perfectly."

"Thanks, but it was nothing, really. I enjoy talking about poker."

I positioned my face into the camera. "Hey, Carl. You might want to get into teaching how to play. Getting Jackson a tournament win was off the charts. I mean, it was crazy."

Carl frowned. "She got lucky, that's all."

Larson said, "You're too modest."

"No, it's true. Remember, anyone can win on any given day. That's luck at play. But if you want to consistently win, you have to own the math behind poker and play with extreme discipline."

I said, "I'm sure it isn't easy. Let me ask you, what kind of person do you think Jackson is?"

Carl frowned. "Well, it's tough to say, as I only know her in one context."

"Come on, you're a pro at reading people."

"I could be off here, but I'd say she seems a bit desperate."

"She dug herself a hell of a financial hole."

"No, I'm not talking about money. It's like Jackson was craving validation in some way. I can't quite put my finger on it, but looking for a position of respect, or expertise."

Growing up in the foster system left scars. "Really?"

"I think so, but her problem is that, rather than do the work to rise to the top, she cuts corners."

"Interesting assessment."

"Look, now that I know what she did, uh, it's ugly, right? But I wouldn't say she's evil or anything like what the press is going on about."

Larson said, "That may be the case, but her record and Nazi-style tactics suggest otherwise. Send me the wire instructions, and we'll get the payment out to you."

"I'll send it right away."

"Have a good trip."

The screen went black. I said, "He's one of a kind. How'd you hook up with him?"

"Tommy knew him."

"Your son went to school with him?"

"Yes. He met him in a computer science class. Carl could create code faster than the professor could."

"I don't doubt it."

"It relies heavily on mathematical equations and concepts to create and manipulate images. Tommy is good at it as well and uses it for the special effects he creates."

"Your son does amazing work."

"These boys grew up with devices in their hands."

I said, "And Carl makes a living without one."

"I never thought of it that way. How ironic."

"You know, I still can't believe Jackson won that tournament. It came out of left field."

"Like Carl said, she got lucky."

"Oh, hold on, a good idea just popped in my head."

55

A TEXT CAME IN FROM MARIO. I PEEKED OUT THE WINDOW; HE was waiting in his car. I put the pistol in my ankle holster and gave a treat to Toby before alarming the house.

Hopping into Mario's car, I said, "How are you doing?"

"Still sober."

"That's not what I was asking."

"Yeah, right. Everybody is waiting for me to start using again."

I slapped his upper arm. "That's bullshit."

He shook his head. "Trust me, you don't know what it's like. People look at you differently."

"I'm not saying some people don't, but maybe you're reading too much into it."

He backed out of the driveway. "Where are we going?"

"Crown Jewelers."

"The jewelry store on Forty-One?"

"Yes."

"Why are we going there?"

"Larson knows the owner."

"And why are we going there?"

"Larson arranged to get something we needed for the Kravitz job, and it's ready to be picked it up."

"I don't mind going, but you needed two guys to pick up some jewelry?"

"It's high value, and for security purposes, you have to be prepared for the worst to happen."

Mario pulled into the strip mall housing a gray, ornate building. I said, "Go around the back."

He parked in front of a door without a sign. We stood in front of the camera and hit the call button.

A lanky man wearing a pink tie over a white shirt cracked open the door. "Come in, gentlemen."

We stepped inside. He locked the door behind us. "I'm Conrad."

As we shook hands, he said, "You know, Larson has been one of my favorite people since we went to law school together. Whenever Ray needs something, I'm happy to help."

"Thanks, you have what he asked for?"

"Yes. Follow me."

We went through a corridor and stopped in front of a door to a safe. Conrad put his palm on a reader. When it blinked green, he tapped on a keypad, a chime rang, and the door clicked open.

The safe was the size of a broom closet. Conrad pulled open a drawer and removed a blue, velvety bag. He locked the door and handed it to me. "Tell Ray I have the certified documentation, and if he needs an affidavit, I'll get one notarized."

"Good. I'll let Larson know."

He stuck his hand out. "Good luck with whatever my friend is up to."

He walked us back to the rear door, checked the camera, and swung open the door. I looked both ways. No one was around. We jumped into Mario's car and took off.

After changing my shirt for the third time, I stood in front of the mirror. Tuck or not? I glanced at the nightstand. Twenty after six. Laura was expecting to be picked up by six thirty.

I left the tail of my shirt out and grabbed my car keys. Driving to her apartment, I kept telling myself everything would be all right. I'd put off going to dinner with Laura's parents as long as I could.

Laura was waiting outside Magnolia Square wearing a lottery-winner smile. She hopped into my Beemer and pecked my cheek. "You're wearing the shirt I got you for Christmas."

I'd forgotten she bought it for me. "Don't say you got it for me."

"Why are you saying that?"

"I don't know. It's just . . . uh, forget it. You look very nice."

"Thank you. I got this at Nordstrom Rack. They only had one, and it was my size."

"You're always lucky."

"You think so?"

"Of course, look who you're going out with."

She shoved my shoulder. "Very funny."

We drove in silence, and when slowing for the light at Golden Gate Boulevard, she said, "You're quiet. Is everything all right?"

"All's good."

"You don't have to be nervous; my parents are the best. They're really down to earth people."

"I don't want to be grilled about what I do for a living."

"Oh, come on, nobody is going to grill you."

"We'll see."

"They may ask, but it's natural. We've been together a long time, and it's, you know, getting serious."

My chest tightened. "What's your definition of serious?"

Her head whipped around. "What? You don't think—"

"Hold on, I was trying to joke around, it didn't come out right."

"Are you sure?"

"Of course, look, I get why your parents would be concerned, but I have a solid, high-paying job."

"They don't care about the money. They just want us to be happy."

That was the standard line, but right after you reached whatever you thought happy was, it was all about the income.

Laura pointed. "There's Mom and Dad."

A white Genesis was pulling into the parking lot for Jimmy P's Charred. I slowed, making sure to catch the red light.

Her parents were sitting at a table under the eye-height fireplace. I shook hands with her father and was given a hug by her mother.

Her dad said, "So glad we finally got to do this."

"Us too, Dad. But Beck has been so busy."

And bingo, she flung open the door, and her father marched right in. "Laura said you're an investigator. What kind, and who do you work for?"

This guy would make a great prosecutor. "I'm independent."

"Commercial or criminal?"

Now I knew where Laura got her questioning skills from. "It depends."

The server took our drink order. Jimmy P's didn't have hard liquor. I ordered a glass of an Italian red wine.

The waiter was barely a foot away when her father said, "You were involved in that case with that drug dealer, Royal. That must have been interesting. What did you do on that one?"

Royal? I wanted to ask Laura to step outside. Her mother

said, "Come on, Frank. Let's not talk about work. It's so boring."

"I was just curious because last time—"

"Dad, didn't you hear what Mom said?"

Before her father could respond, the waiter appeared to tell us the specials. Laura kept the conversation light and off work.

We said our goodbyes and climbed into the car.

Laura said, "You see, that was a lot of fun."

I shrugged.

"Don't tell me you didn't have a good time. You were laughing a lot."

"Why did you tell your father about the Royal case?"

"I didn't. I swear. He must have seen it on the news or something. Remember, they mentioned your name."

"It was just that jerk in the prosecutor's office who said I helped out, and it was gone in a day or two. Your father had to be looking for information on me, he was digging around."

"If he did, he was only, you know, trying to find out about you because we're together."

I nodded. "I know. If I had a daughter, I'd do the same."

"You'd make a great father."

I didn't know about that, but I sure as hell learned what not to do from my foster father.

56

I SWUNG OPEN THE FRONT DOOR. MARIO STEPPED INSIDE, saying, "A suit? Man, you're all duded up on a Saturday morning?"

"Well, for someone whose wardrobe consists of shorts, T-shirts, and one collared shirt, the bar isn't too high."

Mario bent over to pet Toby. "Hey, you forget this is Florida?"

"That doesn't mean you don't have to make an effort. Grab the other side of the coffee table."

We moved it to the side and rolled up the rug. The finger-print reader on the safe blinked green and the door clicked open. I reached inside, pulling out the blue velvet bag.

After closing the door, we put the furniture back in place.

"Get a treat for Toby."

"Sure."

Mario opened the treat drawer, and I grabbed a pair of glasses. I alarmed the house, and we hopped into Mario's car.

The lights in the storefront for the Kravitz campaign were off. The door was locked. I rang the bell, and Kravitz stuck his head out of an office. He raised a finger, and a second later the door buzzed. I pulled it open and headed to the back.

"Representative Kravitz, it's good to see you again."

"You as well."

I started to sit, and he said, "I don't have much time this morning. Did you bring it?"

I patted the pocket of my jacket. "Yes, sir."

"Good."

I pulled the bag out and held it up. "Before I give it to you, I want to be sure—"

"My word is impeccable. When I make a deal, I deliver."

"All I'm trying to avoid is a misunderstanding."

He reached for the bag. "Give that to me and I'll make sure your project is funded."

"I want to show you what's inside while we're both here." I lifted the bag and gently shook out a handful of diamonds." I extended my arm. "These are beauties. Look at the way they shine."

"Hurry up, I've got to get going."

Easing the diamonds back into the sack, I said, "Time is of the essence on this. How fast are you going to do this?"

"I have a committee meeting Monday. I'll bring it up then."

"You're going to Washington?"

"Tomorrow morning."

"What kind of committee is that?"

"Appropriations."

"Perfect." I handed him the bag.

Kravitz pulled the drawstrings apart. He looked inside as if I'd pulled a sleight of hand. "I'll be in touch."

The cell on my nightstand rattled, waking me up. It was 2:37 a.m. I grabbed it as Toby hopped off the bed. "Hello?"

"Beck—"

"Mario? What's wrong?"

"I'm sorry to call so late, man."

Was he high? "Are you all right?"

"Yeah, I was laying here. I have a lot of trouble sleeping, you know, always got the monkey on my shoulder."

I put my head on the pillow. "It's okay, man. Call me anytime you feel like you're slipping."

"No, I'm not slipping or anything, I was thinking about you and what happened with Weiss, and I could be mixing things up. In recovery, they told me when something is bothering me to talk about it."

I'd only play therapist at two in the morning for Mario. "That's okay, man. What can I clear up for you about Weiss?"

"Well, remember you told me about the guy between your house and the time you were being followed?"

I swung my legs off the bed. "What about it?"

"I was using a lot at the time, so I could be wrong, but wasn't that before Cindy and the Ritz thing with Weiss? Before the fire?"

Mind racing, I stood. "Uh, yeah. It was—"

"Doesn't that mean it wasn't Weiss's guy?"

How the hell had I missed that?

57

BASEBALL CAP, SUNGLASSES, AND FAKE BEARD ON, I STOOD OFF to the side as Kravitz and his high-profile attorney, Gordon Frost, came out of the courthouse.

The press surged forward, and Frost put up a hand. "The congressman is not going to comment this afternoon. However, I'll make a brief statement concerning today's proceedings."

Four hands holding microphones thrust forward.

A reporter shouted, "How did Congressman Kravitz plead?"

Frost glared at the reporter. "I said I was going to make a statement."

The crowd quieted, and the lawyer said, "Today we forcefully denied the allegations leveled against my client. In fact, we're going to ask the court to dismiss the charges."

"On what grounds?"

"We believe the search of the congressman's home and office were illegal and unconstitutional. As evidenced by the release of Mr. Kravitz under his own recognizance and without bail, we believe the court will look favorably on our motion and rule accordingly."

A reporter asked, "The prosecutor's office confirmed news reports that a bag of loose diamonds was seized during the raid. Why did the congressman have those gems in his home?"

Frost smiled. "I'm glad you asked about that. Congressman Kravitz has a long history of collecting valuables, including gems. We're going to establish and document that undeniable fact. It's important to understand that the hobby of collecting stones, both cut and uncut, has been practiced by the Kravitz family for several generations."

"So, it wasn't for a bribe?"

"Of course not. It is part of the congressman's collection. In fact, many of them were probably passed down from his father and grandfather."

"When is the next court hearing?"

"My office is drafting a motion to dismiss, so we believe it'll be a brief hearing at that. That's all for today."

Kravitz held his head high but stared at the back of Frost's dyed head of hair as they walked through a sea of reporters. He was defiant and had hired one of the best legal minds in the country.

Inhaling, I counted to eight before slowly exhaling. I repeated the process six times, wiped a bead of sweat from my brow and headed to the car. We had enough to nail Kravitz, didn't we?

Stepping into the midday sun, I scanned the area and hustled to my car. Nobody was following me. There was a tiny chance that the threat I had seen by my house was a random burglar. If not, I was back to thinking it was either Mallory or Royal.

My cell rang. It was Detective Moreno. "Hey, Moe."

"Hiya. Look, I checked with every contact I have in the Corrections Department, and we don't have anything concrete on Royal."

"Concrete? What do you mean by that?"

"That wasn't the right word. There's no doubt Royal is still running things from jail, but there's nothing indicating he's running something that's targeting you."

"If that's true, it's got to be Mallory."

He didn't respond.

"Moe? You still there?"

"Yeah. Look, you have every right to be paranoid after what Weiss tried to do, but are you sure there is a threat?"

"What?"

"I'm just saying, with everything that's going on, you've been hyper vigilant. Maybe you misread—"

"There was a guy by the side of my house, man. What the hell do you think he was doing there?"

"Hold on. I don't know what that was about. Maybe it was a thief or somebody casing a house."

"Did you forget somebody was following me?"

"No, but you were messing with Kravitz and Weiss. These guys are going to do their homework—"

"By sending a goon out at night?"

"Beck, take it easy. I'm just saying the tail might be unrelated to the guy at your house."

It was something I never considered. "Sorry, man."

"It's okay."

"I'll ask them to run a regular patrol by your place."

"Thanks."

"Keep your eyes open, and I'll see if any of our informers has anything."

"Thanks, Moe."

Driving home, I thought about the possibility the threat was imagined. Mario always said I was paranoid. And Moe had a good point about the two incidents possibly being unrelated.

My shoulders relaxed. About to call Laura, I palmed the

steering wheel. I'd forgotten about the man at my house while Laura and I were staying in a hotel. There were three incidents.

Mind racing, I recalled we'd gone to Miami after the fire. It could have been Weiss making another attempt.

58

———

I READ THE TEXT FROM O'LEARY. THE PROSECUTOR SAID THE arraignment was the next one up. Slipping into the courtroom, I took a seat in the last row as O'Leary sat behind the prosecutor's table.

Judge Appleton looked at the defendant's table. "Is the defense ready?"

Simone Jackson and her public defender scrambled to their feet.

"Yes, Your Honor."

"Ms. Jackson, how to you plead?"

Jackson mumbled, "Not guilty, Your Honor."

The judge made a note and glanced at O'Leary, who stood. "The state is comfortable releasing Ms. Jackson without bail."

Judge Appleton said, "Noted, Counselor. Two weeks from today, the twentieth, will be the next court date." He rapped his gavel. "Next case."

Head down, Jackson made a beeline for the door. Her clothes hung off her. I stepped in front of her. "You don't want to go out the front, there's more cameras than at the Academy Awards."

She frowned. "Oh, where can I get out?"

"I'll show you. There's a side entrance they don't know about."

"Are you a lawyer?"

"No, but I work for a couple of lawyers."

"On the defense side?"

"Sometimes, and sometimes for the prosecutors. Follow me."

I made a left down a corridor and opened the third door. Jackson stopped at the threshold. "Here? This doesn't lead outside."

"I wanted to talk to you before you left."

She took a step back. "About what?"

"The Dubers, what you did—"

Jackson turned around.

I said, "Hold on. I can help you with the charges you're facing."

"And how are you going to do that?"

"I know Prosecutor O'Leary very well."

"So does my lawyer."

"Not the way I do."

"All right, how much do you want? Because I don't have any money."

"Let's sit and talk about it in private. I'm sure you'll find the deal I'm proposing interesting."

We sat across an oval table. Arms crossed over her chest, Jackson said, "I'm giving you five minutes, so you better get started."

"You're here on bribery and child endangerment charges. But what you did to the Dubers was reprehensible. What you did to them and who knows how many others is twisted and vindictive at best. But you're lucky I know about the extenuating circumstances you've gone through."

"Now you're a therapist?"

"No, but I went through the foster system as well. I wasn't shuffled around as much as you, but I got my ass kicked too many times before taking off before aging out."

"How do you know about me?"

"I'm paid to know. Look, I was in the system. I know it can be rough."

"It wasn't the best way to grow up."

"What I don't get is you knew the system from the inside, and you still did what you did."

"I don't have to explain myself to you. You have something more to say that isn't a sermon? If not, I'm out of here."

"I don't know if it was the gambling that pushed you off the rails or what was going through your head, but you screwed over the Dubers—"

"I was trying to protect children."

"Maybe originally, but you know what I think?"

Jackson started to get up.

"Sit down! You listen to what I have to say, or I'll make sure you rot behind bars!"

Jackson sat. "Who the hell do you think you are to talk to me that way?"

"Because I know why you did what you did. I felt the same way when I first escaped foster care."

"Yeah? And what's that?"

"You wanted to deny kids a normal childhood. You wanted every kid to suffer what you did."

Jackson's face darkened. "You done?"

"You wanted others to feel the way you did. I felt the same way when I was first in foster care and was getting screwed around. I looked at other kids, and I'm embarrassed to say it, but I resented that they had normal parents."

Jackson shifted in her chair but said nothing.

"It could've been the way my mother got killed."

"What happened?"

"She was murdered by a bastard who was out on bail."

Jackson shook her head. "What about your father?"

"He couldn't handle it and drank himself to death."

"At least you had parents. I never even knew mine. You know how that makes you feel?"

"I'm sorry. I know it was devastating, and if it wasn't for that, I wouldn't give two shits what happened to you."

She whispered, "You said you could help me."

"There's a good chance you'll get time behind bars. But for sure, you'd lose your pension on top of your job."

Jackson hung her head. "I really screwed up. I needed the money—"

"I don't want to hear it."

"I know I don't deserve it, but is there any way you can help me?"

"Nothing can be done to reverse the damage you did, but we can try to make some lives better."

"I'd do anything—"

"The money you won from the tournament is frozen as the entrance fee came from the bribery money."

"If I get it, I'll give it to you—"

"I want forty thousand of it to go to the Dubers, to reimburse them for the lawyers you made them get. Then we'll put ten grand into a college fund for their kid. The remaining fifty is going to Youth Haven to help them take care of the kids."

"Whatever you say, I mean it sounds good, and you're really being nice."

"You plead guilty, agree to be banned from working with children, turn over the hundred thousand, and you'll avoid jail time. And we'll work the charges around so you'll qualify to draw a partial pension."

"Really? Oh my God, thank you, thank you, thank you."

"We'll reach out to your attorney to set everything." I stood. "Come on, I'll bring you to the side exit."

59

———

PROSECUTOR O'LEARY MET ME IN THE PARKING LOT AND brought me into a room adjacent to his office. He clicked on a remote, and a monitor came to life, displaying a video feed of his office.

"They're waiting downstairs. I'll have them brought up."

"Thanks. I know it's unusual, so I appreciate you letting me see this."

"You earned it, Beck. I'll see you later."

O'Leary closed the door behind him. Seconds later, he appeared on the screen. The prosecutor picked up the phone and made a brief call.

A minute later, O'Leary said, "Come in."

The door swung open. Congressman Kravitz and his lawyer, Gordon Frost, stepped in. They exchanged greetings and sat in the shamrock-green chairs in front of O'Leary's desk.

Frost said, "I was heartened by your phone call. The congressman is anxious to get this misunderstanding behind him so he can get back to doing the people's business."

The reference to public service made me gag.

O'Leary said, "Since you submitted the motion to dismiss, I thought it best to avoid any embarrassment."

"Though the illegal search deserves a public humiliation, the congressman's interests lie in a quick and quiet resolution."

"Excellent, shall we get started?"

Kravitz crossed his legs as his attorney said, "I know it wouldn't reflect well on your office, but when you drop the charges, you really should make a public statement. As a public figure, it's the least we can ask. You can find a way to cast blame on the police—"

"Mr. Frost, let me be clear, we have no intention of dropping the charges."

Kravitz uncrossed his legs and looked at Frost. The lawyer said, "Is there another misunderstanding?"

O'Leary smiled. "None whatsoever."

"What is the meaning of this meeting, then? You said you wanted to keep this—'low profile' was the phrase you used."

"That's correct. Though the charges are as serious as they come, I'm offering you a chance to change your plea to guilty."

Frost stood. "This is a waste of our time. We'll see you in court."

As Kravitz rose, O'Leary said, "I wouldn't do that. You'd lose, and your client would be publicly humiliated."

I leaned in as Frost said, "I'd say it will be your office who'd be disgraced."

"Please sit. It'll only take a moment. I want to show you something."

"We'll stand. What is it?"

O'Leary picked up a remote, and a TV came to life. It was the recording of the meeting I had with the congressman in Baker Park.

Kravitz said, "I was being filmed? Without my consent?"

Frost said, "My client has a reasonable expectation of privacy. This will be thrown out of court."

O'Leary said, "This was taken outside his office, in public. No consent is needed as there is no expectation of privacy in the middle of a county park."

Frost protested, and the prosecutor said, "Hold your objections until I play this for you."

Kravitz and I were face-to-face. "As I've said, the idea of providing a safe haven is close to my heart, and I'm more than willing to help you convince your colleagues it's an urgent need."

Kravitz scanned the area before saying, "Incentivizing them would be an expensive endeavor."

"We understand."

"How much are you prepared to spend? I need to spread the money around."

I liked the way I had leaned into him. "For a ten-million-dollar grant, you get a hundred thousand. If you can swing twelve million, I'll up it to a hundred and fifty."

Kravitz smiled. "A hundred for ten million? That's one percent. It hardly qualifies as a finder's fee."

"What do you want?"

"Three hundred thousand for ten, four hundred if I get twelve million approved."

I hesitated. "Sounds fair, but getting that kind of cash is a problem for me, and frankly, it'd raise flags."

"I can handle it, but it's crucial we stay under the radar."

"It'd be tough. What I can get my hands on are diamonds."

"That's an interesting idea. I've never used them before."

"I use them all the time. They store tremendous value in a small package."

"I'll have to think about that."

"Trust me, they're used all the time. The feds don't track them like they do cash."

Kravitz nodded slightly. "Okay. I'll give it a go."

"Good. When will you get on it?"

"I'll have some upfront expenses. There are some people I need to take care of. I'm going to need an advance."

"How about ten grand."

"Make it twenty, and that has to be cash."

I stuck my hand out. Kravitz shook it, saying, "Good doing business with you."

O'Leary stopped the tape.

Kravitz shook his head. "This is entrapment, plain and simple." He turned to Frost and said, "Get this thrown out as entrapment. Immediately."

Frost put a finger to his lips.

O'Leary said, "That's not going to work, Congressman. You asked for compensation in exchange for funding his project. It's a classic quid pro quo."

Frost nodded and lowered himself into a chair. "Let's discuss this, keeping in mind that people say things, like they want to kill someone, but never take action. Mr. Kravitz may have misspoken, but no money was received by him, and no deal was consummated."

"Surely you haven't forgotten the diamonds, have you?"

Kravitz collapsed into a chair as his lawyer said, "Those were owned by the Kravitz family decades before this unfortunate incident."

O'Leary smiled. "Nice try, Counselor." He opened a folder on his desk and slid a sheet of paper to Frost. "This is a list of the serial numbers engraved on the gems found in the congressman's home."

Kravitz's shoulders sank, and O'Leary held up another document. "That list matches up with the inventory record provided by Crown Jewelers, who lent the stones to law enforcement."

Frost exhaled. "We're going to need to examine these for authenticity—"

"You're going to need to speak to your client about a plea."

"If you provide us with a fair offer to consider, we might be able to come to an agreement."

60

Laura grabbed my hand as the Gulf lapped at our feet.
She said, "This is nice. We should walk on the beach every
Saturday."

"We got to get out early like today."

"That's fine by me. You're the sleepyhead."

I wasn't a late riser. It wasn't sleep that kept me quiet and
leery of booking early morning appointments. I liked to read the
papers and go over the plans I had in motion. "Let's make a
date. Saturdays, no later than nine, our feet hit the sand."

"Wow. You sure you can handle that much of me?"

I hadn't thought it through. It meant we'd probably be
together the entire day. "It'll be a test."

My phone rang. It was Larson. "Hey Ray, I'm taking a walk
on Vanderbilt Beach with Laura, are you here yet?"

"Nice. No, I have too many errands to run today."

"What's up?"

"Can you talk?"

"Sure."

He hesitated. "They found Melvin Weiss dead this
morning."

I stopped in my tracks. "What?"

"He hung himself off his balcony. A housekeeper saw him when she went in this morning."

"Oh my God, this is terrible."

Laura said, "What's the matter?"

I shooed her away as Larson said, "I guess he couldn't handle the disgrace."

"I fucked up."

"You didn't do anything. He—"

I said, "Bullshit. Weiss wouldn't have killed himself if we didn't go after him."

"Take it easy. You have no idea what was going on in his head before you even met him. These things don't come out of thin air."

"I got to go. I'll call you later."

Laura said, "Weiss committed suicide? Who is he?"

I plopped onto the sand. "What a disaster."

"Weiss? The man who tried to kill you?"

I grabbed a fistful of sand and flung it at the Gulf. "Argh!"

Laura sat beside me. "Relax. What's done is done."

She'd spat out some stoicism. "Yeah, and a man is dead because of me."

"You're exaggerating, aren't you?"

"Fine, you want to know why I think it was me, I'll tell you."

Her eyes widened as I told her about the Weiss case.

"I'm not saying he should've killed himself, but he was a terrible man. He set your house on fire—"

"People can always get another job, but when you're dead, you're dead."

She rubbed my back. "The creep made his wife look like a fool."

"She was divorcing him. This is so fucked up."

"I don't know why you're so upset. This man tried to kill you."

"That doesn't make a difference."

"Are you crazy? Of course it does. It shows was a monster he was. He had no regard for anyone. He was as selfish as they come."

"And now he's dead because of me."

"He committed suicide. People don't just wake up one day and kill themselves. He probably had mental issues, demons he was dealing with, way before he met you."

Larson had said the same thing. "You think so? I mean, I'm sure we pushed him over the edge, but you might be right."

"You don't know what else was going on behind the billion-dollar facade Weiss put out there. And the guilt he must have felt for the way he got his money had to be eating at him."

"Maybe."

"Don't blame yourself. You were supporting the people Weiss hurt."

I stood. "Let's get going."

She grabbed my hand, and I pulled her to her feet. She put her arms around me. "Don't let this bother you. Shake it off. You're a good person and are not the reason that man took his own life."

I wanted to believe it but had serious doubts. "Thanks."

We walked in silence for about ten minutes. Passing The Turtle Club, my phone rang; it was Larson again.

"Ray? What's up?"

"I just hung up with O'Leary, and he told me Solenko made a deal and turned the state's evidence against Weiss. You weren't the only guy he targeted."

"Did Weiss know he snitched?"

"Yes. O'Leary reached out to his lawyer late yesterday."

I felt lighter as relief washed over me. "So, that's why he hung himself."

"Yes, and O'Leary said the SEC was looking into Weiss as well."

"His world was crumbling."

"It sure was."

"Thanks for letting me know. But why didn't O'Leary tell us?"

"His daughter was playing soccer and tore ligaments in her ankle. He rushed out of the office."

"Oh, no. Is she all right?"

"He said the surgery went well."

"Good. I'll call him later."

I hung up and said, "The guy Weiss hired to kill me cut a deal with the prosecutor and dished up a ton of dirt on Weiss."

"See? It wasn't your fault."

It may not have been, but I had a role and didn't like the way the movie ended.

61

I called my detective friend Moreno. "Hey, Moe, how is it going?"

"Good. What about you, everything quiet?"

"Yes. I heard what you said the other day, and I'm not going to let it dictate my day-to-day. I'll keep my eyes open, and we'll see where it goes."

"Attaboy. We'll keep the patrols going and our ears to the ground."

"Thanks, hey, I called to invite you out to dinner, my treat."

"I can pay my own way."

"Not this time. If it wasn't for you, Weiss would've put me in a casket. So, dinner it is."

"It's not necessary."

"Look, pick a place. Nothing too fancy, but a place you and your wife like. It's about time we double-dated."

"Wow. I'm finally going to meet the mysterious Laura?"

"Don't bust my chops, or I'll retract the invite."

He chuckled. "We were going to go out Friday. So, I know that night works, but you choose the restaurant and let me know."

"Sounds good."

Ten minutes later, Laura arrived. She breezed into the house with a Whole Foods bag. "They had turkey burgers on sale."

"Good."

"They were fifty percent off. I'm going to make a salad."

As she pulled open the fridge, I said, "Look, Friday night, we're going out to dinner with Detective Moreno and his wife."

Burgers in hand, she froze. "Friday?"

"Yes. Why, do you have plans or something?"

"No, no. Just, I don't know, I'm a little surprised."

"You'll love him. He's great, and his wife, Tammy, is funny as hell."

"Can't wait. Where are we going?"

"Where would you like to go?"

"Me? It's not up to me. Anywhere is fine by me."

"How about Bice?"

"Sure."

"I'll put the grill on, then make a reservation."

I fired up the barbecue as a text came in from Larson.

After dinner, we cleared the table. I put the TV on, navigating to WINK News. Laura said, "I thought you didn't like to watch the news."

"I don't, but Ray wanted me to see something."

A pest control advertisement ended, and the newscast started. The anchor said, "Tonight's lead story is a fall from grace."

A picture of Kravitz filled the screen. "Congressman Kravitz was unanimously censored today by the House of Representatives. The censor is related to the bribery charges filed against Kravitz.

"The congressman's committee appointments were also revoked, and reports are circulating that Kravitz will resign as soon as this weekend.

"The Congressman—"

I clicked the remote. Laura said, "Why did you want to see that?"

"We did some work with him."

"I read about him. He's so corrupt."

"We thought so."

"What did you work on with him?"

"Come on, Toby needs to go for a walk."

Laura was sleeping. I lay in bed ruminating on everything that had happened. As bad as the Weiss suicide was, I felt pretty good. Instead of breaking my balls about what I had done, Laura supported me, helping me to rationalize what happened.

Maybe things between us could go to the next phase. If I was going to have a kid, I couldn't let much more time pass. And she had the right values to make a great mother.

My mind drifted to work. I'd probably have to change what I did; I couldn't risk someone coming after me when I was a father.

The threat, real or imagined, had receded. Nothing unusual had happened, and I was able to relax a bit. I thought about Larson.

He had a couple of interesting jobs to consider.

I wanted to take a breather, go away with Laura, and stay off the radar for a little while. Being with her felt good, but I had to remove any doubt that she was the one, and time revealed everything.

But the cases Larson told me about were time-sensitive and lucrative. Eyelids getting heavy, I vowed to make a decision by the weekend. I scrunched up my pillow and shut down my thoughts.

Laura and I were sitting on the lanai. I was reading the paper when the sun peeked over the trees. I said, "Look at that sky. It's going to be another beautiful day."

Laura smiled. "That's why they call Southwest Florida paradise." She got up. "You want another cup of coffee?"

"Sure." I handed her my mug, and she went into the house.

She stuck her head out holding a phone. "Somebody is calling."

I took the cell from her. "Hello?"

"Mr. Beck, it's Jim Duber."

"Oh hey, how are you?"

"Good, good."

"And Katy?"

"She's great."

"What's up?"

"We wanted to thank you. We didn't expect anything, but I can tell you, getting that forty thousand back is beyond belief, and the ten thousand for Katy's education, I mean, we don't know what to say."

Larson had put the extra ten grand up. "We're just glad to help in any way we could."

"It means the world to us, believe me."

And the universe to me.

The Thrilling Sequel in the Art of Payback Thriller series

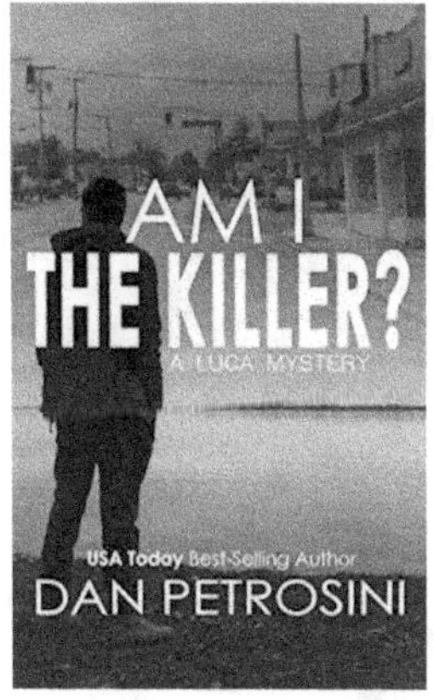

Am I the Killer? - A Luca Mystery Crime Thriller-Prequel

Enjoy another thrilling series.

start reading book one of Suspenseful Secrets, **CORY'S DILEMMA.**

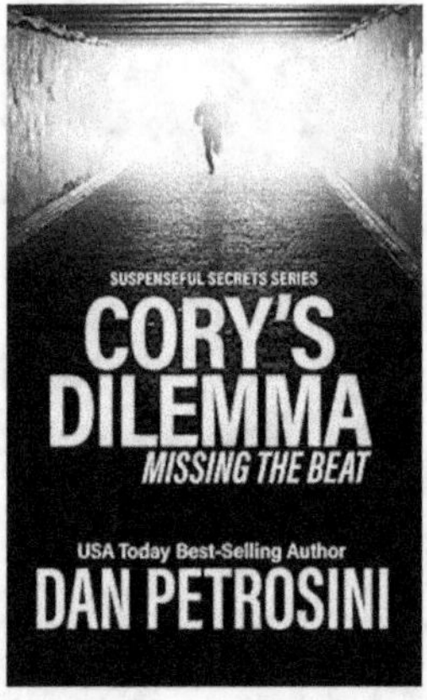

His big music career break . . . was because of a lie.

<u>**The Luca Mystery Series**</u>

Am I the Killer

Vanished

The Serenity Murder

Third Chances

A Cold, Hard Case

Cop or Killer?

Silencing Salter

A Killer Missteps

Uncertain Stakes

The Grandpa Killer

Dangerous Revenge

Where Are They

Buried at the Lake

The Preserve Killer

No One is Safe

Murder, Money and Mayhem

<u>**Suspenseful Secrets**</u>

Cory's Dilemma

Cory's Flight

Cory's Shift

<u>**Art Of Payback**</u>

Race To Revenge

Beyond Revenge

ABOUT THE AUTHOR

Dan is a USA Today and Amazon best-selling author who wrote his first story at the age of ten and enjoys telling a story or joke.

Dan gets his story ideas by exploring the question; What if?

In almost every situation he finds himself in, Dan explores what if this or that happened? What if this person died or did something unusual or illegal?

Dan's non-stop mind spin provides him with plenty of material to weave into interesting stories.

A fan of books and films that have twists and are difficult to predict, Dan crafts his stories to prevent readers from guessing correctly. He writes every day, forcing the words out when necessary and has written over twenty-five novels to date.

It's not a matter of wanting to write, Dan simply has to.

Dan passionately believes people can realize their dreams if they focus and act, and he encourages just that.

His favorite saying is – "The price of discipline is always less than the cost of regret"

Dan reminds people to get the negativity out of their lives. He believes it is contagious and advises people to steer clear of negative people. He knows having a true, positive mind set makes it feel like life is rigged in your favor. When he gets off base, he tells himself, 'You can't have a good day with a bad attitude.'

Married with two daughters and a needy Maltese, Dan lives in Southwest Florida. A New York native, Dan has taught at local colleges, writes novels, and plays tenor saxophone in several jazz bands. He also drinks way too much wine and never, ever takes himself too seriously.

He puts out a twice-a-month newsletter featuring articles, his writing and special deals and steals.

Sign up at www.danpetrosini.com